Clelia

When Love Died: A Tale of Sorrows

Philip Antony

Cover Illustration by Mackenzie Rose Ridgeway

For my beloved Sara Jean —

My editor, best friend, and soul mate

Acknowledgments

I wish to thank the two people who contributed to bringing this story to fruition. Special thanks to Claire Cieslewicz, for her interest in the project, for her reading and editing the first draft. Many thanks also to my dear friend, Roberta Frisoni, for helping me to understand the Vatican organization and its politics. Both Roberta and Claire are former teachers, whose numerous edits spared me any embarrassment owing to my grammar and spelling deficiencies.

It is with enormous gratitude and sadness that I acknowledge the contribution of Sara Jean who was my first and most critical editor; who helped with the numerous re-writes; and who gave me the encouragement to continue to write not only this story, but also many others. Sadly, she is no longer with us, and will be missed as my best editor, friend and life partner.

Table of Contents

Chapter 1

March 17, 1878. It was a typical March morning in Rome - neither winter nor spring, just a constant drizzle in the mist, making the day cold and miserable. The normally busy Via del Corso, where both people and horse-drawn carriages vied for space whilst hurling abuse at each other for perceived traffic transgressions, was nearly deserted. On such a bleak day, only a few of the bravest or foolhardy tourists could be seen, all with dour faces but determined to make the most of their visit – one more checkmark on someone's "bucket list."

It was a faint knock on the old wooden door that aroused a somnolescent Sister Philomena from her duty as *monitor della porta* (the door monitor). It wasn't so much a knock as it was a more hesitant tap. At first, Sister Philomena thought she was imagining it; she wanted nothing more than to return to her early morning stupor. "Tap, tap" and then nothing. She silently cursed her misfortune at being assigned to the graveyard shift at the door. She was, after all, one of the senior members of the order of the Poor Claires. One of the novices should have been appointed to the early hours. She would see Mother Superior in the morning about this indignity.

She eased herself out of the wooden chair and trudged slowly to the door. This was the only door that opened directly onto the streets outside the Vatican. There were no Swiss Guards or other security guards to protect the nuns. This was a thinly veiled gesture to the public that the sisters, and hence, the Church, were available to everyone in need. Sister Philomena opened the door that seemed to resist her attempts - a bad sign. It squeaked and moaned as she used her rather significant weight to open the door. As she did so, at her feet lay a rough-hewn wooden basket that could only signal one thing – yet another unwanted child from some despairing woman caught in the web of an unplanned, unwanted, or forced pregnancy, unfortunately so common these days. She peered into the cold morning haze to see if she could call out to the mother to convince her of the evil of abandoning a child and to plead with her to reconsider her decision. But there was no one. The mother had made her decision. The child was now *un Cittadino Vaticano* (a citizen of the Vatican or a Vaticana).

Sister Philomena quickly picked up the baby and hurried along the dark corridors, lit only with candles, to Mother Superior. Abandoning all protocol, she banged on the door.

"Mother, Mother, please, someone abandoned a child at the door. What should I do? Please tell me."

To Sister Philomena's surprise, she heard an angry muffled voice asking, "What sex is the child?"

The old nun was momentarily stunned, but she knew why the question mattered. Again, came the voice of an agitated woman on the other side of the door, "What is the sex of the child?"

"Just a moment," replied the nun. She quickly unwrapped the swaddling to discover that the child was a girl. She replied, *"Una piccola ragazza"* (a little girl).

Mother Superior opened the door. She was completely dressed as she would be during the day. Sister Philomena thought to herself, *doesn't she ever sleep in night clothes? Is this what it is like to be a mother superior?*

"Come in," the superior nun commanded. "Is the child white, healthy and with all her limbs?"

"Yes, Mother, she is wet, but appears to be healthy and hungry judging by her cries."

"Very well, go to the commissary, and feed her some warm milk; and get her some dry swaddling." Just as the nun turned to go, Mother Superior added, "And notify the Swiss Guard. I have told them repeatedly to put a guard on that door. We cannot afford any more *bambini abbandonati* (abandoned infants). Our orphanage can only accommodate just so many. I will notify the Cardinal Secretary of State. Now go!"

After feeding and dressing her, Sister Philomena carried the baby, now happily asleep, to a small children's ward that resembled a hospital nursery, except that all the babies were healthy girls. It was here that this newly found bambina started her remarkable life as a 'Vaticana.'

The nurse in charge there, Sister Immaculata, was a tall, gaunt woman with a sallow face, pallid from her lifelong appointment in the nursery – there was little time for anything else but for looking after a room full of crying baby girls. Despite her appearance, the elderly nun was compassionate and gentle, like a grandmother, who loved her job. Sister Philomena rushed breathlessly into the nursery, "Sister Immaculata, sister, I'm afraid we have another guest."

The nun looked over to the nun holding the child, and stretched out her arms.

"Poor thing, let me have her. You have done well, Sister. I'll give her a warm bed, food, and the blessings of our Lord and Savior."

Sister Philomena handed the child over, and as her shift was over, she quickly returned to her cubicle for a long nap.

Sister Immaculata's entire world was the nursery, a large windowless room painted in a bland institutional shade of tan. It was filled with ten small cots for the older children and five cribs for infants, the last one to be occupied by the newest resident of the Vatican. An alcove in the nursery was the extent of Sister Immaculata's personal world. It consisted of a single bed, a small side table with a reading lamp, a chair and a small chest of drawers. On the wall, hung the obligatory crucifix, and pictures of various saints, including the founder of the order, Saint Claire. Despite the sparse surroundings and monastic décor, Sister Immaculata loved her simple life together with her fifteen infant charges whom she called her *bellissime margherite* (beautiful daisies).

Within moments of Sister Philomena's departure, Father Domenico Giancarlo, the Cardinal Secretary of State, entered the nursery accompanied by four priest attendants and Mother Superior. Upon seeing the Cardinal, Sister Immaculata rushed over, fell to her knees and kissed his extended hand.

"Good morning, Your Excellency, how may I be of service?"

The rotund cardinal had a ruddy complexion, an easy smile and a gentle manner. He resembled more a chef in one of the many "pizzerie" that were scattered around Rome. He walked around the room blessing each of the children and touching them on the forehead, saying, "Il Nostro Signore ti ama. *(Our Lord loves you)*."

Upon completion of his round, he approached Sister Immaculata, "Show me the child that came to us this morning."

"Here she is, Your Excellency."

"What a beautiful child. Is it not sad that these children will not know the love of a father and mother? But no matter, she will enjoy the love of Sister Immaculata, her sisters, and our Lord and Savior."

Not accustomed to such recognition, Sister Immaculata blushed.

The Cardinal Secretary of State looked at both nuns, "I presume that she has not yet been baptized. Then, let us prepare to protect this child from the evils of Satan."

The new baby remained peacefully asleep throughout the baptism. As the ritual ended, the cardinal said, "Let us give a name to the newest member of our Church." He looked around, "Any ideas?"

Mother Superior spoke first, "Shall we call her Clelia in honor of the patron saint of our order?"

"Excellent! So be it!" the cardinal announced cheerfully. He turned to one of his priestly secretaries, "Kindly enter her name in the register of citizens of the Vatican."

And so began the life of Clelia, as a Vaticana.

Chapter 2

Clelia's early life was austere. There were neither children's games nor sports – just prayer and chores in the service of the Church. She was raised by the nuns not as a child, but more as a future novice. Each day began the same way: rising before dawn with prayers and going to an early morning mass attended by all the nuns, and officiated by the Pope himself – the one privilege that the children had. There were prayers before and after every meal, followed by the chores that the children called, *faccende da schiavo* (slave labor). These daily chores consisted of washing floors on hands and knees to doing laundry by hand for the numerous religious persons who lived behind the walls of Vatican City. During these labors, the children prayed aloud, asking for forgiveness for their misdeeds and minor peccadillos. Notwithstanding these public revelations of sin, their lives included weekly confessions of sin and professions of faith. Many of the children were terrified when entering into the dark confessional to be confronted by a threatening disembodied voice speaking through a wire mesh screen, "What sins have you committed?"

So often, a child needed to be physically pushed into this black box, screaming and kicking; so great was their fear. Once in the confines of the box, the little girl, who was eight now, had to concoct sins lest she received a menacing remonstration for her silence, "What? No sins? None of us are without sin. Are you?"

"No, father, no. I am a sinner. Why just this morning, I ….."

"*Bene! Dire un rosario ogni giorno. Ora vai con Dio,*" came the almost jubilant ghostly voice, telling them, "Say one rosary every day. Now go with God."

The relieved child rushed to her room. She had peed herself.

There was no education to speak of, just basic Italian and reading, taught using the Bible as the sole reference. Equally, there was no love, compassion, or warmth in her life besides the occasional encounter with Sister Immaculata. Her life was a mundane spotless existence – more of a monastic one than a childhood.

Chapter 3

It was before dawn when the nuns and the fifteen girls assembled inside the chapel to await the arrival of Pius IX. After an hour of continuous prayer and chanting, the Pope and his retinue finally arrived. Immediately, silence fell. The Pope's assistants hurriedly prepared the altar for the simple daily mass. Unlike the high holy days when the full weight of the Catholic Church's grandest pomp and ceremony were on display, this was a private mass for the Pope and his little orphans.

It started out as any other daily mass that the Pope shared with the children, but this day would change the lives of everyone, especially the little orphans. As the Pope reached that part of the mass called the "Elevation," he raised his arms, holding a piece of bread that was to become the body of Christ. At that very moment, he rose several feet, and was suspended there until the brief prayer was recited, which the children would later testify to as well.

Upon witnessing such a spectacle, the nuns cried out, "A miracle, a miracle!"

At the conclusion of the elevation prayer, the Pope resumed his position, apparently unaware of what had happened, and continued conducting the mass. However, the children were dumbstruck. No one made a sound. They looked at each other as if to say, *"Are you seeing what I'm seeing?"*

In the Catholic tradition, during the hearings to determine the canonization of a person to sainthood, the church fathers must produce at least two miracles after the candidate's death. The proponents submitted that the elevation of the Pope was one miracle to be credited to

Pius IX. The opponents to sainthood, known as the "Devil's Advocate," argued that whereas the miracle of the Pope's elevation had occurred during his life – all saint's miracles were recognized after death as was the historical precedent – and should therefore be excluded from consideration.

These hearings, often contentious, included the testimony of the fifteen children who witnessed the alleged elevation. Each child was rigorously interrogated as if in a criminal trial. While the older of the fifteen were not too phased, the younger ones were completely baffled by the questioning, many of which went as follows:

"Do you know how old you are?"

"Do you wear glasses?"

"How long have you worn glasses?"

"I'm standing 10 feet away; now 20 feet; now 30 feet. Can you see me clearly?"

"What time did you rise this morning?"

"What were you doing between the time of rising and the alleged event?"

"You must have been sleepy; I know I can get sleepy with all those prayers so early in the morning. Were you sleepy?"

"You want to please the good sisters don't you?"

"Did the good sisters tell you to say that you saw the Pope rise up off the ground?"

Despite the harsh interrogation, what could not be shaken or contradicted was that the children unmistakably witnessed the Pope's elevation.

Over the objections of the Devil's Advocate, the reigning Pope, John Paul II, the final arbiter of sainthood, declared that the elevation was so extraordinary that it should be considered a miracle for Pius IX's canonization.

*[Note: Pope Pius IX was beatified on September 3, 2000.]

Chapter 4

March 17, 1896. The orphanage was run by a strict order of ascetic nuns whose lives were devoid of maternal love. There was no warmth, neither support nor compassion for the fears confronting a typical little child alone at night with a room full of other little girls who were also terrified of the demons of the night. In their later years, the children recalled that the only physical contact they had with the nuns was from corporal punishments at the hands of the nuns for the slightest breach of *le regole del buon ordine per* *promuovere la sanita* (the rules of good order to foster holiness).

Deprived of any maternal guidance, Clelia, now a budding teenager, learned that her periods were 'dirty' and a curse brought about by the Original Sin of Adam and Eve. Indeed, she had no idea of the meaning of *mestruazione*. It was only at night in the confines of their dormitory did the girls even utter the word "sex" in hushed tones. To do otherwise would most assuredly have led to fierce retribution from the nuns.

Clelia's life was built on ancient rituals, prejudices, and practices – all devoid of human attention and affection. Life was to be one of servitude, devotion, penance and sacrifice – a journey to salvation.

By the time of her eighteenth birthday, Clelia had become withdrawn, angry and morose. Her animus with the orphanage, the nuns, priests and anything associated with the Vatican had only grown with every passing year, reaching its culmination as she turned eighteen. She struggled to maintain her relationships with the other girls. She had no friends to speak to except a girl named Carla, a gentle soul who was the one person to whom Clelia confided, albeit reluctantly.

"Carla, I am eighteen now, so I have decided to leave the Vatican. It is suffocating me here. There must be a world outside of these walls where I can breathe the fresh air of freedom."

Carla looked at her friend dolefully, "I admire you, Clelia, your courage and determination. I do not have your strength. I think I shall remain a Vaticana here in the safety of these walls. I have only a year left before I too must decide on my future."

Clelia knew that at the age of eighteen, every orphaned child there was required to choose: to leave the orphanage, or to continue as a novice and become a nun herself. With no one to consult or to advise her on the enormity of her decision, she chose to leave the world into which she had lived for all these years with a mixture of fear and anxiety. She had never been outside the walls of the Vatican. Her world had consisted of 110 acres of Vatican City, most of which was off-limits to the children.

On the morning of Clelia's eighteenth birthday, March 17, after mass, she was summoned to Mother

Superior's office for 'the talk' where she would be asked the dreaded question: would she stay or would she leave? Clelia knocked on the nun's door, and heard, "Come in, child."

"Good morning, Mother Superior, God bless you, Mother Superior." Clelia approached the nun who was seated on what could only be described as a throne. She knelt before the nun and kissed her ring.

"Sit, sit, child."

After a few moments of silence, Mother Superior spoke, "This is a special day, Clelia. It is the day we celebrate your birthday, the day you came to us, as a blessing from God. Since this is the day you have turned eighteen, you must make a life choice. Do you wish to stay here with your sisters to embark on the journey as a bride of Christ? Or do you wish to leave the Vatican?"

To Mother Superior's utter shock, Clelia did not hesitate at all with her response as she quietly pronounced, "I wish to leave."

"Is that your final choice, Clelia? You know once you leave, there is no returning."

"Yes, Mother, I understand. I wish to leave."

Mother Superior's tone turned ice cold. "So be it. Pack your things. You will leave immediately."

Clelia rose from the chair. She approached the nun's chair to offer a final kiss to her ring. However, in an act of retribution for her choice, Mother Superior withdrew her hand, saying, "You may leave."

Clelia curtsied, turned and left.

With only a cloth bag with wooden handles, she took a final walk down the well-worn corridors towards the door. There was no one in sight. All of the other girls were performing their chores. No goodbyes, hugs, kisses or promises to see one another again. As she approached the door monitor, the nun could tell, at the sight of the girl's bags that she was leaving the orphanage. Not a word was spoken: no 'arrivederci,' no 'Good luck.' The nun simply handed her a small purse with only enough money to get a room and something to eat, opened the door, and slammed it shut as Clelia stepped out.

And that was it. The conclusion of eighteen long years behind Vatican walls. She turned around to take one last look at the door she was carried through eighteen years ago as an *abbandonata* (abandoned) and now leaving much the same way. Nothing had changed in her life except that now she had been left to her freedom, a freedom for which she was totally unprepared.

Clelia had no idea where she was in the city. She walked along in the shadow of the massive walls of the Vatican until she reached the Via di Porta Cavalleggeri. She walked slowly, looking left and right, inhaling her freedom. *Amazing! What a feeling of lightness and joy!* she thought to herself. As it was still early, carriages and pedestrian traffic were light, so her walk across the Ponte Principe Amedeo Savoia Aosta was pleasant and quiet. She stopped midway on the bridge, leaned over the rail, and stared hypnotically at the Tiber River flowing slowly, elegantly under the bridge. How much water had flowed under this bridge since she was born? Who was she really? She thought, *my life thus far has been like the flotsam flowing under this bridge.* Fear welled up in her, *what if I made the wrong choice; what will become of me? I have no skills except prayer and service, service and prayer. What will I do? Who will look after me?* The questions kept flowing with the water under the bridge.

She did not remember how long she had spent at the bridge railing. Her reverie was interrupted by the chaos of the growing morning traffic. The business of the day had begun. She walked away from the railing and continued crossing the bridge until she reached the Corso Vittorio Emanuele.

She was so overwhelmed with the sights and smells of Rome that she didn't realize how long she had been walking along the Corso. It was late in the morning when she felt the need for something to eat as she had not been able to have breakfast before leaving the Vatican orphanage. She spotted a small café but was reluctant to walk in for fear of being perceived as an escapee from an institution. She waited for a couple to walk in and then followed them to the counter.

"May I have a cappuccino and a croissant for two please," the gentleman asked.

"That will be 9 lira, please."

Clelia stepped up, plucked up her courage and asked for the same. The irritated server asked her to repeat the order, "Speak up, I can't hear you."

She realized that she was looking down at her feet and whispering, but this is what one did when speaking to the nuns, a priest or a person of high rank. "Do not look the sister in the eye, and speak only in a respectful tone, and then only when spoken to." This was one of the *regole* (the rules).

Clelia looked up and asked for the order again. The server looked at the young woman closely. Her close-cropped hair, her simple, unstylish dress and her reverent manner told him that this was not the usual patron. She was somehow different. He softened his tone, "Of course, miss."

Clelia took her breakfast to a quiet corner, reflexively made the sign of the cross and silently ate her meal. Breakfasts were not for socializing but for silent prayerful reflection and thanksgiving to God for the gift of a new day. That's how Clelia had begun every day for the past eighteen years. She realized that for the remainder of her life, the orderly existence from her years in the convent would change, but she could not know then just how drastic that change would be.

It struck her that all of the needs that she had assumed for all these years would always be provided to her would now be her sole responsibility. The first order of business was to find both a roof over her head and a job. The priority at this moment was the roof. A short distance from the café was a rather run-down four-story building with a sign for rooms to let. She entered the hallway, and after an awkward interaction with a large woman in a disheveled yellow floral print dress, completed the transaction: the rent to be paid weekly, no meals, no noise, no gentlemen guests. Surprisingly, Clelia found the room, which overlooked the Corso, to be light, a bit worn, but otherwise livable. She set her things down, and went to the side of the bed and fell to her knees to pray her rosary in thanksgiving to God for His protection and for getting her this far on her first day of independence.

After completing her rosary, she took off her clothes except for her underclothes and slipped into bed. Later, she woke up startled and realized that she had been sleeping for several hours. The sun had slipped past her room, that was now cast in the shade. She was hungry and decided that instead of going to a new café, she would return to the earlier one.

The man behind the counter recognized Clelia as soon as she walked in the door.

"Ah, miss, "What can I do for you?".

Again, casting her eyes down and speaking *sotto voce*, she asked, "May I please have a ham and cheese sandwich?"

Feigning a stern look, the man behind the counter reminded her, "Miss, speak up, I can't hear you."

Clelia picked her head up, "I am sorry, sir."

The man smiled benevolently, "My name is Felice. What is your name?"

Hardly above a whisper, eyes cast down, she responded, "Clelia."

Felice came from behind the counter. He was a tall man with enormous hands, a thick neck and muscular forearms. His hair was an unkempt mass of curls. He noticed she was still wearing the clothes she had worn in the morning. He smiled and said gently, "Again, please. A little louder."

Clelia was momentarily frightened as this giant of a man approached her. She looked up at the man. Despite his imposing size, he had a kindly face, flowing white hair, and a gentle voice. She had to imagine that he was a priest. She repeated, "Clelia, signore."

"No, not 'sir,' my name is Felice, please."

She responded with a bit more emphasis, "Clelia, Felice, my name is Clelia." Then, she lifted her head and repeated her request with even more emphasis, "May I please have a ham and cheese sandwich, Felice?"

Felice responded, "Of course, Clelia."

As he returned to the counter, he added, "What a lovely name!"

He noticed that she looked frail, thin and pale. Her dark hair was short and straight as if cut by a wool shearer. Her clothes were simple but worn-out, similar to a factory worker or a person working in the bowels of a hospital. Her shoes were more like slippers, certainly not sturdy enough to keep out the cold or rain. And yet, despite her situation, she had a gentle demeanor.

As she stood there waiting for her sandwich, Felice saw her eyeing the food in the display case: the different kinds of cheese, meats and salads. He could tell that she was starving. He then prepared a sandwich that seemed to her more the size of a football. She looked wide-eyed at the enormous sandwich. She thought to herself, *this is enough food here to feed three nuns.* "How much?"

"For such a good customer, it is free."

Clelia walked back to her flat, confused by Felice's generosity but happy that her first day was such a success. After eating only a portion of her football-sized sandwich, Clelia prayed the rosary in thanksgiving for her good fortune. In bed that night, she fell asleep imagining what the other orphans were doing.

Chapter 5

One does not forget the habit of 18 years. She arose at sunrise, got to her knees at the side of the bed and began her morning prayers. She asked for God's guidance as she began the second day of her new life. Dressed in a drab grey shift dress provided by the convent, she went to the café for breakfast. Not waiting for other patrons to pave the way for her, Clelia entered and asked Felice, "May I please have a coffee and a croissant, Felice?"

"Buongiorno, Clelia," Felice wished Clelia a good morning as he handed the coffee and the croissant to her.

"What are your plans for today?" He then added with a knowing smile, "What would you be doing today in the Vatican orphanage?"

Clelia was stunned. He knew! But how? Is that obvious?

"Don't be ashamed or concerned. You are always welcome here."

For Clelia, it was now or never; she summoned her courage and asked, "Felice, I need a job."

They discussed her skills, which were limited. Whilst in the convent, as a girl, she was only taught domestic skills: cooking and housekeeping. Girls who were not otherwise entering the convent were expected to be married and have as many future Catholics as possible.

Felice and Clelia agreed that there weren't many jobs available for a "refugee" from the Vatican orphanage. Clelia could not accept such a dismal future. She was all the more determined to find a job, and if nothing else, prove the nuns wrong: there was a life after the Vatican.

The next morning after her morning visit to Felice and the café, Clelia walked the few streets to the National

Central Library of Rome. She spent the next four weeks learning shorthand and typing. Every day without fail, she would turn up at the opening of the library at 9:00 am. She was there just as the custodian was unlocking the doors. She would spend the entire day reading and practicing her shorthand. The chief librarian took pity on this waif, and let her practice her typing on one machine in the basement of the museum.

Several times during the day, she would emerge from the basement to listen to conversations in order to practice her shorthand. Her typing skills were improving by the day. Not long after four weeks, she had mastered typing at 65 words a minute and had a working knowledge of shorthand.

She stopped at the café one late afternoon to announce to Felice that she was ready to start her job search. He had become not only a mentor, but also the father figure that she never knew, and Felice was happy to play that role for her.

"I'm ready," she announced as she walked in. She told him what she had learned.

He put his arms around her and gushed, "Wonderful, Clelia. I'm so proud of you!

For the first time in her life, she felt human warmth. Initially, she stiffened – and he did sense it immediately – and then she leaned into it. What a wonderful feeling! She now had a father, a person who was proud of her and what she had accomplished. I will never let this feeling go. She held on to him for the longest time.

She was overwhelmed, surprised, thrilled and exuberant with herself at this momentous encounter. She released him from the embrace, and stepping back looked him in the eyes and said, "Ever since leaving the Vatican, you have been a father to me, one that I never had." Speaking in child-like innocence, she asked with the purity and directness of a child, "May I call you Papa?"

Tears welled up in Felice's eyes. This was not the time to tell her that a long time ago, he had been a father to a beautiful girl, Gina; and that she and his wife, Antonia, were both killed by a drunken driver. Gina would be Clelia's age now. But now, by a quirk of fate, he had acquired – dare he think it – a daughter, not one who was fleeing from parents, but one who had no parents. It was a perfect match. God has given me a gift, another chance at fatherhood.

Seeing the tears in his eyes, Clelia apologized, "I'm sorry, I didn't mean to offend you."

"Offend me? You beautiful girl, I am thrilled beyond words. Of course, I would be honored to be your papa."

"Papa, would you help me find a job?"

"Yes, of course," replied Felice.

They spoke well into the night trading ideas about job opportunities: waitress – no, not for a former Vaticana; a housekeeper – no, too much like life in the orphanage; a teacher – a good idea in principle, but she could only teach Bible studies. What about a secretary? Yes, that might work. She could type and knew enough shorthand to get by. They looked at the job listings in the Rome newspaper, *Corriere della Sera*, for secretarial opportunities. The bold color advert screamed sensual pleasure: "Piazza Navona Tours & Tickets." It showed tropical beach scenes with umbrella-topped drinks and scantily clad young girls cavorting in the sea. Clelia's eyes widened. She had never seen anything like this. It was hypnotic. "Papa, this is the one!"

Felice rolled his eyes and shook his head. This was not the time to be protective. Oh well, how harmful could a travel agency be? It didn't require a great deal of business experience and minimal typing skills. It certainly wouldn't be difficult for Clelia to put airline tickets together and make hotel reservations.

"Well, if that's what you want, you have my blessing."

Chapter 6

Early the next morning, she arrived at the café for her usual breakfast with Felice, now Papa. On the coffee counter, she saw a box with a large red bow on top, and a slip of paper that read, "Good luck!" Felice was standing behind the counter, smiling broadly. He gestured toward the box. "Open it"

"For me?" She approached the box with trepidation; she had never received a gift in her entire life. She stopped in front of the box, both elated and anxious. Slowly, almost deliberately, she unwrapped the gift as tears welled in her eyes. She separated the wrapping paper to find a plaid skirt and a lovely white blouse with ruffles.

"You can't go to your job looking like an orphan."

With tears streaming down her cheeks, she said, "My God, they're beautiful!" She ran around the counter and threw her arms around Felice, "Thank you, thank you."

"Quickly, change," Felice urged.

Clelia ran around the counter into the toilet and slipped into her new clothes. The only evidence of her humble beginnings were her shoes that she hoped no one would notice.

As she emerged from the toilet, he exclaimed, "You look beautiful."

"Do you think so, Papa? After all, I don't look like those girls in the advert."

Spoken like any father, Felice responded immediately, "Thankfully no, you are lovelier than they."

Complete in her new outfit, Clelia started out for the Piazza Navona Tours & Tickets office with a confident stride. She followed Felice's written directions, and within a few short minutes, found herself at the door of the travel agency. On the front door a sign read, "Help Wanted."

Unlike her first encounter on her first day out of the orphanage, Clelia opened the door and peered into a dimly lit, suffocatingly small office. Despite the depressing environment, it was a beehive of activity. There was one lone desk that was piled high with papers. "I'm here for the job," she said to no one in particular.

An elderly woman stood up and approached her with an air of authority. It quickly reminded Clelia of Sister Superior. She shuddered.

Dispensing with any formalities, the woman said brusquely, "Can you type? Do you know shorthand? Can you start now?"

Clelia took a deep breath, and mustering all of her confidence, responded with equal brevity, "Yes, I can type, take shorthand, and I'm ready now."

The Sister Superior look-alike looked at the young woman up and down. Again, it reminded Clelia of Sister Superior on one of her morning inspections of the girls' living quarters. Apparently satisfied, the stern-looking woman directed her to a desk piled high with papers, files and detritus from that morning's coffee and brioche. She issued vague instructions on Clelia's role, then turned and went back to her desk, leaving Clelia to figure it out for herself. A test perhaps? It didn't take long for her to navigate the simple filing system, and by noon she had completed most of the filing. Throughout the remainder of the afternoon, the travel agents dropped files and paper tickets on her desk without so much as a "please" or "thank you." Clelia forced a sweet smile at each person. She kept pace with the flow, and by the end of the day, all but several files were in their respective cabinets.

At precisely 6:00 pm, the Sister Superior look-alike commanded to everyone in the room, "We're done for the day. Go home." As she walked out, she looked over her shoulder to Clelia, "Tomorrow at 8:00." Clelia took that to mean that she had a job. She was about to ask about compensation, but the woman turned and walked into the evening crowd.

The streets were beginning to buzz with diners, buskers, jugglers, and street-corner musicians. Clelia negotiated the crowded streets taking in the smells, the music, and boisterous pedestrians hurrying to begin the evening. At one corner, she stopped and closed her eyes. How wonderful! She was jolted out of her reverie when a young man engrossed in his newspaper bumped into her. "Sorry, miss." She smiled at the same time, realizing that she had just encountered a man that was not a priest. It was momentarily confusing, but she surprised herself with a breezy reply, "It's quite all right." She turned and crossed the street. The smirk on her face said it all, *I did it, I did it!* She wasn't quite certain of what the "it" was, but it felt good nonetheless.

Buoyed by the encounter and her new status as a working girl, she rushed to the cafe to tell Felice all the wonderful news. Although the café was bustling with a queue waiting for a table, he greeted her with a large hug that nearly took her breath away.

"Papa, I have so much to tell you!" She didn't wait for a private corner; she burst out the good news of the job and the brief encounter with the stranger and her reaction. Given the crowd at the café, her conversation was overheard by quite a few diners. To her shock and embarrassment, they began clapping and cheering. "Congratulations, congratulations."

One of the diners closest to Clelia asked her name.

"Clelia, sir."

At that point, the man rose to his feet and called out to the other diners, "Everyone, Clelia has a job. Let's toast her good fortune."

Felice stood back to let the adulation wash over her. She covered her face and started crying, overwhelmed by the attention. This was all so new. Felice put his arm around her as she hid her face in his massive shoulder. He then announced, "My daughter and I thank you. Yes, we must celebrate. A glass of wine for everyone!"

For the remainder of the evening, Clelia was the main attraction. Patrons came up to her, planted a kiss on each cheek and wished her good fortune. Felice took her around several tables to introduce his daughter to his better customers. All the men at each table rose to congratulate her with more kisses on each cheek. This was all so new — men acknowledging her for just being her. She didn't need to lower her eyes or kiss anyone's ring, or be ordered to clean a room. Although she felt a growing sense of confidence, she still held tightly on to Felice's hand.

Clelia had left the convent orphanage with just her given name. No one knew or even bothered to investigate further. She was just Clelia, the orphan girl, "la Vaticana." Now, she was Felice's daughter. Out of respect for Felice, no one enquired about the details of his newly found daughter. After years of unhappiness at the loss of his daughter and wife in a tragic car accident, a dark cloud seemed to have lifted this evening; Felice was happy and that's all that mattered. She had become Clelia Tessarini, daughter of Felice Tessarini, owner of a successful Michelin three-star café.

Later that evening, alone in her room, she stared up at the ceiling, reminiscing about her day. The reminiscence then turned into an unsettling soul-searching. *Is this what my life will be like? I am so fortunate to have Felice, but will he always be there? Am I really free? I have no real social skills. I am living a solitary life similar in many ways to my life behind the walls of the Vatican, but without the cruelty of the nuns. Will there be more to life yet to come? And how would it reveal itself? Are these feelings of emptiness, fear, and loneliness just part of my new life? Does everyone have these feelings?*

She puffed up her pillow, turned over and within minutes was asleep.

Chapter 7

The days and weeks turned into months. Her life became a routine of a morning coffee with Felice, then the travel agency, back to the café, and then home. However simple her life, it was her own. She had not yet found happiness in her new life, but rather a sense of purpose beyond those dictated by *la regola* (the rule). *But then, what is happiness?* she thought. *Was it an abiding sense of purpose and completion, a harmonious connection with life with all its travails and triumphs? Am I already happy and don't know it?*

She had become an indispensable member of the travel agency. She knew more than anyone in that office about how the business worked, where all the files were, and the government agencies that regulated the business. She realized that she was particularly adept at keeping financial records. In effect, she had become the administrator of the business second only to the owner, the mother superior of the agency. Members of the staff recognized her growing status and importance to the functioning of the business. They no longer simply dropped files off on her desk. It was now, "Thank you, Clelia" and "Please, Miss Tessarini."

It had been a typical day at work. At precisely 6:00 pm, the owner and Mother Superior look-alike announced the end of the workday. The agents rose as one and filed into the street, leaving only Clelia who was evidently engrossed in her accounts. In a voice reminiscent of her Mother Superior look-alike, the owner raised her stern voice, "Miss Tessarini, we are finished!"

"I am sorry. I was just finishing today's revenue figures," as she jumped up from her desk.

Hearing that, the owner softened her tone. "Thank you, Miss Tessarini."

As she walked along the now familiar streets, she once again felt a slight thump on her shoulder. She immediately recognized the voice, "Sorry, miss." Unbeknownst to her, this was no accidental encounter, but how could she know? Unlike the last encounter, she reacted simply by nodding. She found herself confused and a little frightened. True, she was accustomed to the encounters in the café, but this was different. This was deliberate and without a purpose that she was aware of. So why had this man made this clumsy encounter?

"We meet again. My name is Vincenzo Talarico. What is your name?"

"Clelia" was all that she was willing to offer. She knew that such an encounter on a busy street was not proper for a young lady.

"May I walk with you? Just a pleasant walk with such a lovely young lady", the young man pressed

She only gave him a sidewise glance. The reply was quick and terse, "No, we have not been properly introduced."

Undeterred, he continued to press his case all the way to the entrance of the café. Felice was speaking to a diner when he saw his beloved Clelia. He broke away and gave her a big hug. She looked alarmed, and when Felice saw the young man standing nearby, he knew why. He released his daughter and walked menacingly with fists clenched, "What do you want?"

Felice towered over the young man, who backed away and raised his hands in a sign of surrender and said, "I'm very sorry sir, I meant no harm."

Felice turned away, put his arm around Clelia, and walked into the café. "Are you okay, my darling?"

She was shaking. This was something new, unexpected and frightening. Such things would never happen in the convent, she thought. But this is the world I have chosen for myself.

He poured some brandy into a shot glass. "Here, take a sip. I found that a little brandy calms the nerves."

She drank the entire glass in one go. She felt like a liquid fire had been poured down her throat – reminiscent of some medieval torture she had read about in the convent. Her eyes were bulging; she clutched her throat and began coughing. Felice tried hard not to laugh. "My darling, I said a sip, not the entire glass."

In a strangulated voice, "Papa, I'm going to die!"

Felice offered her a glass of water that she eagerly took. With a chuckle, he said gently, "Well, at least you're not afraid any longer."

Clelia scowled as she continued to clear her throat. Felice covered his chest with both hands in a sign of remorse, "I'm sorry, my darling."

Chapter 8

It was Christmas in Rome, the time when all of the city was decorated with lights. Every shop window was resplendent in white lights, candy canes, and plastic Father Christmas faces inviting shoppers to spend. And then, it seemed that every apartment balcony was awash in colored blinking lights; each apartment trying to outdo its neighbor with the numbers, colors and dazzling arrays of ornaments. This was Clelia's first Christmas. She helped Felice decorate the café. It was a mass of glittering-colored lights, sprigs of pine, and loops of crepe paper. Christmas carols played in the background. *My first Christmas,* she thought. *What joy!* She had difficulty concentrating at the office. She was so excited to return to the café and immerse herself in the Christmas ambiance. True, this was the birth of Christ, but rather than celebrating the joy of His birth as in previous years, she had spent the night in the dark, solemnly praying and intoning Gregorian chant and the Latin Mesa Cantata (the Mass Sung in Latin). The café, in all its splendor, represented for Clelia the most wondrous celebration of this special day.

Clelia rushed to the café to find an enormous Christmas tree in the middle of the room. Felice's café had become, for many in Rome, the place to launch the Christmas festivities. The size of the tree took her breath away. Its fragrance permeated the room.

"Merry Christmas! Felice spread his arms to embrace Clelia, who seemed overwhelmed.

She pressed her hands to her lips, "It's…it's so beautiful."

Felice beckoned, "Come quickly, my darling, we need to string the lights before our guests arrive."

He explained to Clelia that it was his custom during Christmas to invite his guests to take a bauble and hang it on the tree. Clelia listened intently as Felice sang traditional songs, songs about Babbo Natale *("Father Christmas")*, reindeer and sleighs, good cheer, peace, Bethlehem and the birth of Jesus. She had never heard such music in the convent. There was no place for such frivolity in the convent. Felice motioned to Clelia to mimic his words and the melodies. She nodded and stumbled her way through the music and lyrics as they both laughed. For Clelia, it was energetic and loud laughter, a feeling that she had never experienced before. They completed stringing just as the first customer walked in, and joined in the merriment with hugs, air kisses and "Buon Natale" greetings.

The twinkling tree lights, the baubles, the decorations, the music and the festive atmosphere captivated her. She went up to Felice and said, "I can't believe that this is really happening to me and I'm here with you. You made all this happen. You have brought joy to me, Papa, and judging by our customers, to them as well."

As if on a silent cue, the customers broke out into typical Italian Christmas carols. They had not gotten through the first few when directly outside the café they heard the unmistakable *zampognari* (traditional Christmas bagpipers and flutist) dressed in conventional sheepskin and wool cloaks playing Christmas carols. Felice went out and brought out a bottle of Sambuca to thank the players and to wish them "Buon Natale."

The dinner and celebrations went late into the night. After more hugs, air kisses and *Buon Natale,* Felice and Clelia were left with a dining room that looked more like a war zone.

"Leave it, my darling. We'll do clean up in the morning when the staff gets here. I have something for you."

She looked at him, puzzled. Felice took her hand and led her to the enormous Christmas tree that continued its quiet and cheery mission, blinking and twinkling. With all the commotion during the evening, she did not notice a pile of boxes underneath the tree. She assumed that they were part of the decorations.

Felice beckoned for Clelia to sit at the table nearest the tree. "Happy Christmas, Clelia. These are for you."

She was at a loss for words. She looked at the boxes with a mixture of disbelief and excitement. "Really Papa? For me?"

Felice nodded and said, "Go ahead. Open them."

The gift boxes were beautifully wrapped with Christmas motifs and a red bow on each. Clelia was almost afraid to open them. They were just beautiful to look at under the tree. Felice handed her the first box. "Open it."

Slowly, she undid the wrapping, meticulously folding it and putting it aside with the red bow. When she opened the box, she gasped. In it was a pale blue silk blouse with a dark blue bow tie on the collar. She picked it up and held it against her - testing the size, but really waiting for Felice to comment.

"Beautiful!" he exclaimed as he clapped his hands.

The next was a very large box. She followed the same process when opening this box: a pair of thigh-high black leather boots. This elicited screams of pleasure, disbelief and joy.

Felice was tired after a long day, but not Clelia. She had forgotten the careful, obsessive folding of the paper and the bows. She now tore at each box with peels of screams, laughter, tears, hugs and kisses. There were boxes of skirts, shoes, a handbag, and sunglasses. But for Clelia, the biggest prize of the evening was a floor-length dark blue wool coat. She was nearly submerged in a sea of wrapping paper and boxes, but it was not the end. Felice had left the best for last.

"I have one last gift for you," as he reached under the tree. This box had no Christmas wrapping paper, no colored bows – just a box. But the box itself could have been a gift. It was made of lustrous rosewood with a gold latch. On the top of the box was a small cross. So highly polished was the box that Clelia could see a dim reflection of her face on it. Thinking that box was the gift, Clelia said softly, "Papa, it's beautiful. I will treasure this always."

"I think that you should open it," as he motioned to the golden latch.

Despite the flurry of activity opening gifts with the accompanying exclamations, somehow Clelia realized whatever the contents of this box, it would be momentous. At first, she hesitated; she was actually afraid to open it. Slowly, ever so slowly, she opened it to find a red leather-bound Bible complete with gold leaf pages and a jewel-encrusted cross on the cover. For several long moments, she was spellbound. There were no words that she could utter to express herself. With tears streaming down her face, she threw herself into Felice's arms. She cried, really cried, for the first time since leaving the convent.

"Happy Christmas my dear," he whispered.

She couldn't help herself as she started to turn to pages to read her favorite passages. For several long moments, she was transported back to the morning chapel services led by the Pope himself. Despite the presence of the nuns, who were armed with a birch switch that guaranteed that none of the girls would fall asleep during the mass, it was, for Clelia, the best part of her long day. There was absolute silence as the Pope read passages from the Bible in Latin. What joyful moments!

Felice sat quietly as Clelia emerged from her reverie. She looked over at him; she could see that he was exhausted. "I'm sorry, Papa; I know you must be tired. If you wouldn't mind, I would like to stay up and read more. I have missed my Bible."

"Of course, Clelia. Don't stay up too late. We have a long day tomorrow. Remember, it's Christmas."

"Yes, Papa, I'll be up shortly." Several months earlier, Felice had converted one of the rooms in his apartment above the café into a bedroom for Clelia. Except for a plastic statue of the Virgin Mary and a Crucifix above her bed, her room resembled her room in the orphanage, where decorations were seen as blasphemous. On more than one occasion, Felice encouraged her, "This is a young girl's room, not a monastic cell. You should decorate it."

Clelia felt her eyes getting heavier as the Bible Psalms began to blur together. After making several trips to carry all her gifts, she entered her room, fell to her knees, and prayed, thanking God, not only for the gifts but more for the gift of a loving father. As she pulled up the coverlet, she glanced around the room, and whispered as she turned out the light, "Papa, you're right. I need to decorate this room."

Chapter 9

In addition to her job at the travel agency, Clelia had made it a daily practice to help Felice serve customers, then close the café, clean tables, and count the evening's take. Felice was occupied cleaning the kitchen. He looked over at his beloved Clelia as she wiped tables and swept the floor, and thought God had given him a gift. He also knew that time was not on his side. She was maturing, coming out of her convent shell, and finding her way, albeit slowly, in the world. He worried for her. Perhaps, it was the convent, her genes, or just realizing that she came into the world abandoned, denied love, and utterly alone but for him. And what would happen if he were gone? *I'm no young man,* he thought. He pushed the thought aside as he heard, "Papa, I'm done," Clelia called out. "Between cash and dinner credit, we did well today."

Felice remembered the young man who wanted to walk with her. His eventual gain would be my loss. Clelia caught the sad expression on his face, "Papa, are you alright? You look unhappy."

Felice walked over to her and put his arms around her and said simply, "I love you, my child, you are my treasure."

She stepped back and looked into his eyes to see the momentary sadness that Felice quickly changed into a warm smile with a hastily crafted question, "Do you know that I have no idea when you were born? What a terrible father I must be."

"No, Papa, absolutely no. My birthday is March 17, the day I was abandoned at the convent door, and the day I left the convent."

"My goodness, then you have been here for a year. Next week is March 17. You have accomplished so much. I'm so proud of you."

Clelia blushed at the compliment. *Yes, it has been a remarkable year,* she thought. *So much has happened. My days in the Vatican seem so far away in a distant universe.* "Thank you, Papa, it has been the most wonderful year of my life. I have a job, a wardrobe with beautiful clothes, my own room, and best of all, God gave me the gift of a father."

Clelia's birthday party in the café turned into another Christmas-like affair. When she was at work, Felice had organized several friends to help him decorate the café. There were streamers, balloons, and papier-mâché festooned throughout. A quartet was warming up for Clelia's arrival. And once again, one table was piled high with gifts from friends, guests and, of course, Felice.

Clelia strolled back to the cafe, unaware of the party that awaited her. As she caught sight of the café in the distance, *that's strange,* she thought, *this is the beginning of the dinner hour, and the café's lights are off.* She hurried her step, and found it odd that the front door was also wide open. As she rushed into the dining room, the lights went on, the quartet struck up the universal "Happy Birthday" accompanied by largely off-key patrons and the clapping. Clelia stopped dead in her tracks, dropped her bag, put her hands in front of her mouth, and looked around in shock. A camera flashed, and then another, and another. Tears welled in her eyes as she stood there frozen in that spot. She scanned the room urgently, looking for her anchor, her rock. Felice, as if on cue, emerged and put his arms around her, "Happy Birthday, my love." Then, with a grand sweeping gesture, he invited each of the diners to echo his birthday wish.

Much like the earlier Christmas celebration, this one went on well into the morning hours, fueled by copious amounts of wine followed by bottles of Limoncello. Diners departed with hugs and kisses for Clelia, who was still stunned by the evening's events. The Carabinieri (the Italian police) had now stationed themselves outside the café to ensure that the celebration ended without incident. After all the guests had departed, Felice invited them in for a late-night piece of cake and sweets to accompany them through the long early hours.

The gifts were piled high, waiting to be opened. Pointing to gifts, Felice pleaded, "I know that today is your birthday, but do you think we could do it tomorrow? I'm exhausted."

Clelia put her arms around her father, "Of course, Papa. It extends my birthday one more day."

"Then good night, my love. "Again, happy birthday. I wish you many more."

Clelia leaned over and gave her father a kiss on the cheek, and said, "There is no way to thank you for this day. I will never forget it, and never forget the most precious gift of all, the love you have given me."

Chapter 10

Summer in Rome was akin to standing in front of a blast furnace. The heat was all-consuming. Romans had emerged from the workplace and were enjoying a rare early evening breeze. It was evening by the time Clelia left work carrying an armload of files. She had proven to be an intelligent, hard-working employee that the others had come to rely on with their issues, both personal and business. She was promoted from a desk clerk to the office administrator responsible for the files, the agents and the finances. Despite the heavy load, she was enjoying the sights, smells and sounds of Rome. Office workers mixed with tourists. This was her favorite time of day. She forgot the stress of work, and was looking forward to going home, dinner with Felice, and a small glass of blackberry brandy with her papa in the late evening.

Her reverie was broken when she heard, "Good evening, Clelia," as the young man passing her said with a nod and a smile. Unlike her previous encounter, she replied confidently, "Good evening, Vincenzo." Surprised by the reply and the confidence in her tone, he turned toward her. Undeterred by the previous encounter, he asked again, "May I walk you home?"

"Yes, you may, but only if you carry these files."

"What do you do that you need to carry all these files?"

"I am the office administrator for Piazza Navona Tours & Tickets. And you, Vincenzo, what do you do?"

"I am a legal clerk in the office of the Minister of Justice."

As they approached the café, Felice caught sight of Clelia and the boy whom he recognized from the last encounter. Felice walked out of the café to meet this interloper, but before he could issue a threat, Clelia said, "Papa, this is Vincenzo Talarico. He is a legal clerk in the Ministry of Justice, and the person who offered to carry my files home."

Felice looked long and hard at this boy, who could feel the penetrating and not entirely welcoming glance. He held out the files to Clelia, but it was Felice who took them. "Thank you, Vincenzo," he said abruptly. He turned to Clelia and motioned him toward the door. She turned to the bewildered young man, "Good evening, Vincenzo, my father and I thank you." He took special note of the inclusion of "my father".

Later that evening, after closing and accounting, she said to Felice, "What do you think of Vincenzo? It was kind of him to carry my files."

Felice's reply was terse and brusque, "I would have carried them for you if you had called."

Clelia smiled, leaned over, and put her hand on his, "Papa, are you jealous? That is so sweet!"

Felice merely grunted.

Vincenzo was now a constant on her way home every evening. And every evening, Felice went out of the café to meet them and escort his daughter into the restaurant leaving Vincenzo to stand at the entrance but never invited inside. Despite Felice's unreceptive treatment of Vincenzo, the young man dutifully walked Clelia home now just about every day.

Clelia persisted with the same question about her father's impression of Vincenzo, and until this one evening, it was always met with a guttural sound. However, this evening, much to Clelia's surprise, Felice reached to shake Vincenzo's hand, "Come in, Vincenzo. Be our guest for dinner."

Clelia looked over to a stunned Vincenzo and shrugged her shoulders as if to say, "I don't understand either."

Felice outdid himself over dinner. He served pasta with a Bolognese sauce followed by an enormous veal chop. Clelia demurred after the pasta; Vincenzo cleaned every plate with, "Sir, that was the most delicious meal I have ever had."

However, it was the wine that opened the trap door that Felice was seeking. It was a truism, *"In vino veritas."* ("In wine there is the truth."). Vincenzo started out listening attentively to Clelia speak about her job, but after more than half a bottle of his best wine that the young man drank, the conversation was overtaken by Vincenzo, who was expounding on his legal theories and the sorry state of Italian politics. After exhausting those subjects, he then went on the condemn the traffic in Rome, the pollution, and the uncouth tourists who savaged our precious Roman patrimony punctuating his remarks with his fork.

Felice just listened, and nodded with an undetectable smirk that only Clelia saw.

Vincenzo gave a slurred thank you and "good evening" to his hosts, as he wove his way out of the restaurant.

Felice looked over to Clelia and said, "Now I will answer your question about my impression of Vincenzo."

Without waiting for Clelia to interject a comment, Felice went on, "He drinks too much, talks too much and speaks nonsense on subjects about which he knows nothing. I must say in his favour, however, that he has a heavy fork – he is a good eater."

Clelia stared at her father, but said nothing, but she knew that it was all true. She remembered her days in the convent when the priests regularly drank more wine than necessary at mass, and then again at lunch and dinner.

Felice closed the evening and any further discussion with, "I don't trust him."

Chapter 11

March 17, 1905. Life was good, Clelia thought to herself as she rushed home accompanied by the now ever-present Vincenzo. Felice tolerated Vincenzo despite his mistrust because his daughter was fond of him despite his social shortcomings, particularly the drinking. Today was her 27th birthday and her Papa promised her that this would be a special celebration. After all, she was now more than a quarter century old. Clelia was now a stunning beauty, intelligent, and especially, a very capable businesswoman.

She now managed both the travel agency and the restaurant in the evenings.

As she rounded the corner to the cafe, she stopped short. In front of the building were several police cars and an ambulance. She looked at Vincenzo, "Oh, my God, I hope that no one in the restaurant became ill." When she arrived at the restaurant, the Carabinieri had blocked access to the restaurant. The ambulance door was open, apparently ready to receive a patient. The Carabinieri recognized her immediately; she was now quite well known in the community not only as a tough-minded restauranteur but also as a woman of grace and good humor. She was particularly generous to children who never had to pay for a meal, and to the police and their families who were given special consideration because of their support for Felice over the years. As she tried to make her way in, the lead Carabinieri, Capitano Salvatore Ruggiero, known to Clelia as "Uncle Sal," stopped her by putting his arm around her and shook his head, "No, my dear, you should not enter. It's your papa."

In an instant, she was overwhelmed with a terror that she had never known. "Is he…is he sick, Uncle?" But she could see by the sadness in his eyes that there was more to this. The captain shook his head, "I'm afraid it's worse. Better that you hear it from me. He's gone, Clelia, he's gone. The medics think that he had a massive heart attack and died instantly. There was no pain."

Clelia's knees gave out as she screamed, "Papa, Papa!" The captain held her as she went down. When she woke up, she didn't know how long she was unconscious; she found herself seated in the restaurant with several of the Carabinieri surrounding her. Several of the longer-term customers had also gathered.

"May I see him, Uncle Sal?"

"I'm afraid not, my darling. His body is now in the morgue awaiting funeral arrangements. As you are his only survivor, that burden will fall on you. But all of us in the Carabinieri and your friends here will help you with those arrangements."

"Thank you," is all she could manage. She was exhausted from shock and crying. She looked around and saw the empty restaurant. It was supposed to be bustling now with patrons eating and drinking, a place filled with laughter. It was different now. The dining room looked old, worn and haggard, just the way she felt. *What am I going to do?* she said to no one. *My papa made all this happen. I just counted the money.*

"Uncle Sal, I'm so tired. I'm afraid that I couldn't stand up without falling over."

The Captain of the Carabinieri smiled and said softly, "I've already seen to that. My wife, Sophia, has prepared a room for you. We can go whenever you're ready."

"May we go now?" She stood up with his help, looked around to the solicitous faces, put her hand over her heart and said, "Thank you to all of you."

The Carabinieri escort consisted of three cars with blue lights flashing and sirens screaming in the night. She was greeted by the captain's wife, who scowled at her husband, "Was all that commotion really necessary, Salvatore?" Now in his home, he was no longer the captain of the Carabinieri, but a husband being chided by his wife. "Well, my dear, we wanted to get her here as quickly as possible." Sophia was not done, "Nonsense. I think that you're all little boys playing with toys." She finished by shaking her head, "Men, they never grow up."

Despite the horror of the evening, Clelia couldn't help but smile.

Come, child, let's get you out of these clothes and into a comfortable bed.

Clelia turned to a sullen-looking captain and said, "Thank you, Uncle Sal."

Chapter 12

March 17, 1910. For Clelia, the five years since Felice's death felt like living in a cave deprived of light and air. Her life was upside down: she quit her job at the travel agency; despite his lack of knowledge of the restaurant business, Vincenzo had taken over as the manager of the restaurant and acted as *maître di* dispensing prime seating and service for a backhander. She had fallen from the daily joy of life with Felice, the travel agency and the restaurant, and had descended into deep despair. No one noticed that today was Clelia's 32nd birthday, not that there was any celebration of her birthday since Felice's death. *Just as well,* she thought, *birthdays are for happy times,* and there were no longer happy days – not ever.

She tried prayer but was left angry and frustrated because she could not understand why she had to suffer again. *Hadn't I suffered enough as an abandoned child behind the loveless walls of the Vatican? What more did God want from me? I pray every morning, before and after every meal; I never miss church services; and during my lunch hour, I visit the Church of Santa Maria in Trivio to pray. What sin have I committed to deserve such punishment?* Many questions with no answers.

The restaurant was no longer the profitable business it was under Felice's ownership after it lost its three-star Michelin status and the cache associated with those stars. She had recently been approached several times with offers to buy the restaurant but, in each case, had flatly refused. It was all she had left to remember her Papa and the wonderful years she had spent with him. However, unbeknownst to Clelia, Vincenzo had already opened the door with other investors who were prepared to offer Clelia a quick sale in return for an all-cash deal. One evening after the last diner had left, Vincenzo approached

Clelia with an idea. In an unusual display of affection, he put his arm around her as she swept floors and wiped tables, "My dear, Clelia, I have an idea that I'm certain that you will like."

Clelia was certain that he was drunk. She shrunk away from his embrace. "What is it, Vincenzo, what is this idea that you assume I will like?"

Oblivious to the sarcasm in her voice, Vincenzo began with a smooth and patronizing declaration, "My dear, Clelia, you have been working so hard here, it seems you are wasting your beautiful life as a slave to this place. You deserve better."

Clelia said nothing. She saw that his glassy eyes and slurred speech were all the evidence that she needed to dismiss whatever he was about to say.

Not hearing her comment, Vincenzo continued, "Why don't we consider selling the restaurant to give us time to live like normal people?"

Clelia noted the "we" and "us" but again said nothing, letting Vincenzo carry on.

Assuming that her silence was assent, Vincenzo lied, "I was approached by a group of people who would like to invest in this restaurant. They are prepared to pay a handsome price for this place. And it will help recover the three-star Michelin rating. I think it would be a good idea for us."

There it was again - the "us". The idea of selling the restaurant was abhorrent to Clelia, but silently she had to admit that the restaurant was an all-consuming business, one that she did not feel competent to run the way Felice did. This was his life, his pride and joy; it was baked into his personality, and it was now hers, but she knew that it would take years for her to be Felice's equal. And now that they had lost the Michelin stars, she knew that it would be an even steeper hill to climb. Vincenzo's wheedling, coated in sugar, made it sound to Clelia more like a serpent's hiss.

"First, there is no 'us' and second, I will not sell Papa's restaurant."

Vincenzo was not about to be put off, "Please Clelia, consider what I have just said. I understand that there is no 'us', but for your own sake, for your future, just think about it."

Clelia was furious, "Leave, Vincenzo, leave now." She locked the door behind him and went to her bedroom. It was the bedroom that Felice had made for her. She could not bear the thought of moving into his bedroom. After her prayers, she got into bed, and broke down into uncontrollable sobs. She had never felt so alone as she did now. "Papa, Papa, where are you? Please, help me," she called out in the darkness. It was a while before she fell into a disturbed sleep.

Chapter 13

March 17, 1913. There was already talk of war throughout Europe, and the speculation was that Italy would be drawn in to the eventual conflict. Laughter and gay table conversations were replaced with somber and hushed discussions lest anyone overhear either declarations of loyalty or denunciation of the government. One had to be cautious in these times. There were spies everywhere. Business in Felice's café was declining rapidly as the subject of war and party loyalty made people think twice about dining in public.

Rather than taking the approach that the business was a strain on Clelia, Vincenzo took a different tactic: the impending war in Europe. Despite her reluctance to agree to any scheme that Vincenzo had concocted, she had to agree that an impending war would diminish the business to the point where it would be impossible to continue. One evening after a particularly long day, Clelia sat alone with a small glass of limoncello. Vincenzo did not come to the restaurant as was his usual practice, forcing Clelia to take on the role of the maître di, bartender and receptionist. She had to grudgingly admit to herself that despite his now heavy drinking, he was an affable host whose fawning attention the guests enjoyed.

As if on some silent cue, there was Vincenzo knocking on the door and waving to Clelia. She let him stand there for a few moments waving like a sidewalk clown. When she did open the door, he rushed past her, "Clelia, have you heard? There will be a war. The Kaiser has expansionist designs in Europe, and we Italians will find ourselves in the position of having to choose sides."

Clelia's response surprised Vincenzo, "I don't care; I have a restaurant to run."

Vincenzo, in an unusual outburst, cried, "Clelia, you are either ignorant or naïve. Don't you understand? If there is a war and Italy is drawn into it, regardless of the side, it will be catastrophic. There won't be a restaurant. If there was ever a reason to sell this business and leave, this is it!"

Clelia did not need a picture to be drawn for her. She knew that if there were a war, Felice's restaurant, any restaurant for that matter, would be the first to fall victim. Judging by the expression on her face, Vincenzo knew that his argument had struck home.

Clelia responded acerbically, "Assuming this talk of war is not just limited to you, and your circle of fascists, who would buy this restaurant for the price that I was first offered?"

Vincenzo had her attention. He felt vindicated after all her insults, and now emboldened to press ahead. "True, we may not get the original amount, but we could still make a good profit, a profit that Felice would be proud of." He just played the "Felice" card and saw by her expression that she was taking all of this in. "And furthermore," he went on, "I know a group of investors who would buy this restaurant despite the talk of war. They may be fascists, as you say, but they are not stupid. They are willing to take the risk that Italy will be spared from the approaching storm of war."

He knew that he had won the first round when she said, "I'll think about it." And she didn't take issue with "we".

"Thank you, Vincenzo. I bid you a good night." Vincenzo took his cue and left Clelia to her thoughts. She didn't need Vincenzo's hysterical ranting about an impending war. She was not only an astute businesswoman, but also well-read. She made it a point to listen to some of the guests speculate and debate about the war. Frankly, Vincenzo wasn't telling her things that she didn't already know.

As it was Monday, the restaurant was closed. That gave Clelia time to clean the restaurant, the kitchen and finalize the accounts for the previous week, and to think about Vincenzo's proposition. Managing a restaurant alone was exhausting, both physically and mentally. True, Vincenzo was of some help, but the burden of ownership was solely hers. It had been a long five years, and frankly, the joys of the title were wearing thin. She asked herself, *is this what I want for the rest of my life? Without a true partner, could I do it alone?* And then there was the matter of a possible war.

On the following Tuesday, the restaurant was exceptionally busy. Vincenzo was flitting around the restaurant, glad-handing and enjoying banal conversation with the guests. He was exceptionally garrulous tonight, fueled by the numerous guests who offered glass after glass of wine to listen to him dispense his theories on love, life and marriage, all of which was said loud enough for Clelia to hear, without the exception of the impending war.

The remainder of the week was busy, especially at the 8:00 pm hour, the time when Romans took their evening meal. Clelia was pleased that the kitchen staff was keeping up with the avalanche of orders. She spoke to several of her regular guests, who complimented her on the quality of their meals. And, of course, she kept a careful eye on Vincenzo. For the remainder of the week, after the last guest left, Vincenzo also took his leave. To her relief, he did not raise the subject of the war. But the hiatus did not last.

Saturday turned out to be the busiest day of the week. Clelia had hired several aspiring musicians to entertain for the evening. As it was a relatively warm evening, she had ordered several tables to be prepared outside on the pavement for the guests who were just happy to have a meal and listen to a lively quartet. The evening ended in the early morning hours with the guests singing along. Vincenzo had positioned himself so as to appear to be conducting both the musicians and the singing. The inebriated Vincenzo waved his arms and sang along with the guests. Clelia watched this man, who was more an immature man-child, but she had to smile as he appeared to have the guests in the palm of his hand.

As he left after the last guest heaped praise on him for his masterful "conducting", he turned to Clelia, "See, my dear Clelia, I can make any restaurant work." With a wave to her, he left, leaving her to clean up. Given his self-appointed status as *maître di*, he felt it beneath him to help clean up. She found it curious that he would mention "any restaurant." Was this just the *braggadocio* of an adult-boy or was there a message? She put the thought aside as she went about her chores, including the nightly take. Yes, it was a good evening. Despite all the talk of war, the evening was very profitable, thanks in part to the antics of Vincenzo.

She reminded herself to pay him for his services. Despite her reservations about him, and there was a growing list of them, she had to concede that he had become an asset to the business. She also knew that if she confessed that to him, he would be impossible to manage after that.

After completing her night prayers, she turned out the light and climbed into bed. For a long while, she just stared up at the ceiling turning over her feelings regarding Vincenzo. True, he was a lazy, irresponsible adult-boy, and funny in a clownlike way, but frankly, he was likable. He was always respectful and solicitous of her situation., even though he was opinionated about most things, especially the impending war, the future of the restaurant, and her welfare. She found herself caught between having genuine feelings for him, and at the same time, uncomfortable with his slow interference in her life. She closed her eyes and whispered, "My dear Papa, I need your help. I am confused."

Chapter 14

March 17, 1914. A year had passed, and the talk of armaments production, espionage, and alliances had grown louder and more strident. The threat of war was a looming reality. The assassination of Archduke Ferdinand on June 28th was the touchpaper that would ignite the war that began in July 1914. Italy had initially declared its partnership in the Triple Alliance with Germany and Austria-Hungary, but soon thereafter decided to remain neutral. A strong sentiment existed within the Italian population and political factions to go to war against

Austria-Hungary, Italy's historical enemy. Italy started aligning itself closer to the Entente powers, France and Great Britain. In return for military and economic support, Italy formalized the relationship on April 26, 1915.

The political intrigue, fear and growing paranoia reduced Felice's restaurant to a shadow. There were nights when it wasn't worthwhile to open the restaurant. Clelia reluctantly let several of the staff go. One rainy evening, when the restaurant was barely a third full, Clelia was seated at the table with one of her long-standing customers, a retired army general, Tulio Albanese, listening to his prognostications regarding the war. Albanese, a long-time friend of Felice, had an abiding hatred of the Austrians with whom he had traded various border skirmishes over the years. As she sat listening intently, the irrepressible Vincenzo came bounding in, and without invitation, sat at Albanese's table alongside Clelia. Albanese did not like the young man whom he considered "un playboy" – a blowhard without any real substance. He especially did not like the growing relationship with his friend's daughter.

Vincenzo immediately inserted himself in the conversation, "There is no doubt in my mind that war with the Axis is imminent, and our government should prepare for it. The first order of business is to organize conscription, and then…"

Albanese saw his opening, and was intent on putting this interloper in his place, "Presumably, sir, you would be at the head of the line to volunteer."

Vincenzo was not equipped to parry Albanese's thrust. "Oh, no sir, I believe I am too old, and I have problems with my feet."

Albanese's sarcastic rejoinder went unnoticed by Vincenzo, but not by Clelia. "That's too bad, sir, but you could volunteer for other duties: administration, processing, intelligence, to name a few. None of those activities would put a strain on your feet."

For a moment, an awkward silence fell at the table with Albanese stroking his handlebar mustache and not bothering to hide the smirk.

Vincenzo looked around the empty tables and offered, "I think we should advertise our business, Clelia. I could organize that quite easily."

Albanese could not stand another moment. He gulped down his limoncello, stood up and said, "Clelia, I must take my leave. I bid you all a good evening." He turned and left. Vincenzo was completely unaware of what had transpired.

Albanese's departure opened the door that Vincenzo was looking for.
"Clelia, you see, war is coming. We must act quickly. We can still sell this place, and avoid the oncoming storm."

Clelia was too exhausted from having to do most of the cooking, thanks to the absent head chef. She now faced cleaning up and doing the day's accounts. "Vincenzo, I cannot speak about this now."

"You are quite right, my dear. I will come by tomorrow. Think about what I have said. Good night." Vincenzo got up and waltzed out of the restaurant. Suddenly, he turned and burst out, "I have a great idea for our future." Before Clelia could respond, Vincenzo was out the door.

Chapter 15

It had been raining for the entire week, and together with the talk of war – lately the only topic of conversation – business was not much better than the previous night. There were few tourists brave enough to face the constant rain, and only a few of the regulars trickled in. Although she was a good cook, she was not up to the standards of Felice and his kitchen team. Plates were now being returned half-eaten – not a good sign.

This time Vincenzo waited until the end of the evening to make an appearance. He opened the door and peered in, hopeful that General Albanese was not holding court as he did last evening. Vincenzo walked in without a word, and for the first time to her dismay, he put his arms around her. "You look so tired, my dear Clelia. How much longer can you do this? You cannot stop a war, and you certainly cannot stop this restaurant from failing if we don't act immediately." Clelia was too tired to resist his clumsy embrace and his now familiar harangue about selling the business.

"All right, Vincenzo, tell me what you propose. What is this great idea you have for *our* future?" She put a sardonic emphasis on the "our."

He was surprised by her reaction. There wasn't the usual pushback or postponement. He thought this was the best and probably last opportunity he would have to convince her. "Well, dear Clelia, I propose…" he hesitated for dramatic effect. "I propose that we sell this place and open up a restaurant in the United States, in New York City. My two brothers are already there. They own a pushcart on Mulberry Street selling pizzas, stromboli, zeppoli, and other Italian delicacies. If they could open a restaurant, it would be a success. We could make money and avoid this war. Doesn't that sound exciting, my dear Clelia?"

She remained silent, which he took as an interest in his proposition. He continued, "The money we get for this restaurant would be used as an investment in a restaurant and in a place for us to live. Imagine our own restaurant with a family and a home. How ideal!"

Still no reaction. Her eyes remained firmly fixed on him as if she were trying to pierce any veils of any deceptiveness. After a very long silence, Vincenzo couldn't stand it any longer. "Well, my dear Clelia, what do you think about my proposition?"

"I will think on it," was her terse reply. Vincenzo was so thrilled with her response that he lunged forward and gave her a kiss on the cheek. Clelia smacked him hard in the face. "Don't you ever dare to do that again without my permission! If this behavior is an unspoken price of your idea, there will not be any deal ever. Now, please go."

Although smarting from the slap, Vincenzo was not to be put off now that he had traveled for so long and so far to get her to the point of listening to his idea. "I'm sorry, my dear, I was just excited about the prospect of our venture.”

Clelia was livid. Her face was flushed with anger. She screamed, “Go.”

He got up and as he opened the door, over his shoulder, he said, “It’s a good idea, Clelia, think about it.”

Chapter 16

For the remainder of that week, Vincenzo did not come into the restaurant. Clelia was of two minds: grateful for not having to endure another sales pitch and having to grudgingly admit that it was quiet without him. For his part, Vincenzo could tell that despite her angry reaction, she was thinking about his proposal. How could she not? Stay and endure a war and bankruptcy or join the thousands of Italians migrating to a new life in America?

There was, however, another motivation behind his "idea": Although he had enough money to make the crossing, he could not see himself behind a pushcart with his brothers struggling to make a living in a poverty-ridden ghetto. No, his plan required Clelia's money from the sale of the restaurant, which would put him in a dominant position with his two older brothers. He would own the restaurant, and they would work for him, or they could push the cart for the rest of their lives for all he cared. He had come this far in his grand plan, but Clelia was the key to success. He realized that he needed to put aside any personal feelings, if any, he might have for her. This was business; feelings could not enter into the equation. But he had to admit that his plan to gain or regain her trust would need to spin a web of sweet deceit.

After a week of absence, he entered the restaurant at the opening. It was an entirely different Vincenzo. "May I help you? I can't cook, but I could serve the tables." Initially, Clelia was skeptical, but she was so busy and harried that she accepted. "Thank you, Vincenzo, that would be most helpful."

The evening passed without a word between them except for calling orders. After the last guest left, Vincenzo again offered his help in cleaning. "That's very kind of you, thank you." An hour later, Clelia sat down at one of the tables and, as was her habit, poured a little limoncello for herself. She had brought two glasses and offered one to Vincenzo, who demurred. "Thank you, Clelia. I must go. Good night." And with that, he was gone.

Clelia was puzzled but grateful for the help. For the next week, the same obsequious scenario played out. He would come in to help serve and later clean tables and the floor. Each time she offered him a drink, he turned it down, thanked her, and then left. There was no talk of war between them, although it seemed to Clelia that was all the guests spoke about. It was becoming clear to her that Vincenzo may have been right: the impending war would change everything, including her business.

One night after the last guest had departed, Vincenzo was about to take his leave when she stopped him with a question. "I have been thinking about your idea." Vincenzo nodded but did not address her statement. Instead, he said almost off-handed, "Perhaps, we could discuss that sometime in the future, but I really must go."

Clelia sat for the longest time, nursing her drink, trying to understand Vincenzo's thoughtful assistance but also his apparent dismissal of her desire to discuss his proposal. Vincenzo returned to his apartment, satisfied that he was making progress with Clelia. *Perhaps, another few months, and she will be asking me to help her sell the restaurant and join me in America.* Clelia went to bed confused; Vincenzo went to bed, satisfied that his web was taking hold of her.

Occasionally the restaurant experienced a night similar to the "old days" before the talk of war, but in the main, Felice's Restaurant barely maintained its operation. Suppliers were an unforgiving lot; payment now had to be made in cash on the spot. There was no longer the accommodation they made when Felice was alive. There were days when after paying the various suppliers and the remaining staff, there wasn't enough for her living expenses.

One early afternoon, as the meat supplier was about to make his delivery, he refused to unload the meat and demanded cash before doing so; a bank draft would not do. Clelia offered to pay half that day and the remainder the following day after what she expected would be a good turnover. The driver then turned and left. She called after him but to no avail. As he pulled away, Clelia stood there by the door and cried. Is this what has become of our business? All because of a war?

It turned out that there was a rumor circulating at the fresh food market that Felice's Restaurant was about to go under. Clelia encountered the same reaction from the other suppliers: cash up front or no delivery. She quickly realized that this was the beginning of a headlong rush down a dark corridor that ended in failure, bankruptcy, and the end of her papa's dream. She thought maybe Vincenzo was right all along: sell the restaurant and leave the country in advance of the now certain war.

Clelia was forced to close the restaurant except for weekends. With this, she hoped to cut down on expenses and still maintain a quality business. With the closure came an unintended effect: many of the staff left in order to find full-time jobs. For Clelia, that was the last straw. There was no hope. It was time to speak to Vincenzo.

Chapter 17

May 12, 1914. Vincenzo had been spending his evenings at another café. From what he could see, Clelia's Restaurant was failing. It was no longer open on weekdays, and the weekend custom was sparse. *Yes,* he thought, *the end was in sight. Just a few more weeks, and I shall make my reappearance. No longer will I be the man hat in hand, begging her to see that my idea was right. She will come to me and beg for help.* He sipped his espresso with an equal amount of sambuca and congratulated himself on his strategy: she will come to me begging for help. I want her to admit that I was right all along. I will dictate the terms and she will conform.

Clelia could not understand Vincenzo's sudden absence. Had he changed his mind about his "idea"? Was he pitching that idea to another restaurant? Was he already gone to America? She had come to the conclusion that despite all his faults, she needed his help. She had concluded that Felice's was a lost cause; it was time to get out. How she would go about the sale, when and with whom was something that only Vincenzo could help. It was no longer distasteful for her to work with Vincenzo; it was now a matter of personal survival. She was unmarried, independent and insolvent, not an attractive combination. She went so far as to consider a marriage of convenience with Vincenzo, but quickly dismissed the idea.

Newspaper headlines screamed "War" in Europe. The soon-to-be warring sides were drawn; Italy initially found itself asserting neutrality. Parliamentary speeches on whether to join the Axis or the Allied Partnership consumed entire newspapers. There were daily marches favoring one side or the other. Given Felice's location, many of those boisterous marches passed in front of the restaurant. Clelia watched from the window and was terrified, but now unalterably convinced that selling and leaving was the only recourse. But where is he, she thought? Why hasn't he come now when I need him?

As if he heard her thoughts, Vincenzo emerged out of a crowd of protestors demanding that Italy throw its support behind the Allies. She saw him and ran to unlock the door. She blurted out, "Where have you been? I was getting worried."

Vincenzo's terse remark came as a surprise, "I've been busy."

Clelia was unnerved by his reply, but ignored it, given her state of mind, "I have wanted to speak to you about your idea."

"Which idea, Clelia? I have many I am working on," came the well-calculated reply.

"You know, the sale of the restaurant," she replied.

"And as I recall…emigrating to America, Clelia?"

"Yes, yes, that idea," she replied eagerly.

Vincenzo's trap door was about to spring open. "What about it, Clelia?"

"I think that we should sell the restaurant and go to America." With that, Clelia had unwittingly fallen through Vincenzo's trap door. It had long in the making, but it was about to ensnare his victim to her everlasting regret.

For several long moments, Vincenzo said nothing, which fed into Clelia's anxieties. "You do realize what this means, Clelia? Once this process begins, it cannot be undone. You cannot change your mind. Because you have waited so long to decide, the price will be the price and the sale will be final. Do you understand, Clelia?"

She nodded. "Yes, I understand."

"Very well, Clelia, I will let you know the final details in several days. I bid you a good day." Vincenzo then turned and left, leaving Clelia stunned.

Was this the same Vincenzo I have known for these many years? What has he become? Did I cause this reaction? She remembered the first days of their encounter, his encounters with Papa, his antics in the restaurant fueled by wine and scotch, and his grandiose schemes and plans. But now, he was a different person. All of those years were gone. *I kept putting him off; I treated him with disdain. He only sees me as another transaction. How wrong I was! Perhaps the sale and my emigrating will show him that I cared about him.*

Before retiring to bed, she looked at herself in the mirror. She was still young, independent and knew her way around the restaurant business. As she stared at herself, she re-played her previous thought: *"The sale and my emigrating will show him that I cared about him." Care about him? Care? No, I don't have romantic feelings about him. I will not become a slave to his imperious manner and his plans. I will set the rules, and he will conform. Otherwise, I'll shut the restaurant down, and retire to a convent.* That last thought – the convent – did not evoke the same response it would have 15 years ago. *I have not been with a man; I have maintained my faith; and I have lived by the precepts of the Church. Entering a convent should be an easier transition than moving to America, and avoiding the prospect of daily contact with Vincenzo and his brothers. No, that will never do.* But the question kept gnawing at her: what then? Despite her reservations, Vincenzo's alternative seemed like her only recourse. She would have to wait for his next appearance.

Chapter 18

June 28, 1914. The evening edition of "Il Popolo d'Italia" had a one-word headline that screamed the news: **WAR!** In equally bold print with the accompanying grizzly photograph, it was reported that the Archduke Ferdinand and his wife, Sophia, Duchess of Hohenberg, had been assassinated. This was the kindling that began a flame that swept across Europe. The newspaper called all young men to join the armed forces to prepare to defend the motherland.

For all his bluster and swagger, Clelia had to admit that he was right. She had to act; it was now or never. It had been two weeks since she saw him. It occurred to her that in all the years that she had known him, she did not know where he lived. For her, Vincenzo was a cardboard cutout hanging in the restaurant. Who was he really? She shook her head with the realization that she didn't really know him at all. She was about to make a life commitment to a stranger.

Another month passed without a word from him. She thought perhaps he had made a similar deal with someone else and was now on his way to America. There were daily reports of skirmishes, battles and intrigue that kept her in a state of constant anxiety.

One late evening in July, as Clelia sat by candlelight in the dining room, she heard a knock on the door. It was Vincenzo. It was clear to her that he was drunk. Instead of his usual smarmy greeting, he took only one step over the threshold and said aggressively, "I warned you that this would happen. If you want to sell, and come with me to America, I need to know now right here, right now. I have plans apart from you, but I am willing to put them on hold if you act now. If not, I wish you good fortune and goodbye."

Clelia was in a state of shock. She thought that they could have a reasonable conversation about price, ownership rights, timing, and travel, but it was not to be. She had lost all control. She was now about to surrender everything that she and her papa had built, and enter into a pact with a person whom she did not really know, an irascible drunk and hungry for a resolution. She concluded that this had all the earmarks of a deal with the devil. But what choice did she have? Stay and go bankrupt or go with this man who had all the answers. Still, the decision was a hard one to make on the spot. She hesitated. Vincenzo turned and as he shut the door behind him, he said, "Goodbye Clelia and good luck."

"Wait, wait, Vincenzo. All right, I will do as you asked," she blurted out.

Vincenzo had his back to her when she called out. A crooked smile came across his face, and with an imperceptible nod of his head, he said to him, "Ah, the sweet smell of victory!" He turned slightly, and continuing with the charade, said flatly, "I will be back tomorrow with the necessary papers. Good evening." With that, he walked off into the night.

Chapter 19

July 21, 1914. Clelia sat by a window, watching the late afternoon shadows begin to cover the surrounding buildings. Vincenzo's knock at the door broke her reverie. Reality, in all its harshness, was about to descend. He carried a sheaf of papers.

Without the usual courtesies, Vincenzo launched into business, "My contacts will pay Lira 10,000 for the restaurant and the building.[1] This is a one-time offer. It is on a take it now or leave it basis."

Clelia was devastated. Papa Felice's life work was disintegrating before her eyes, and at this point, she felt helpless to do anything about it. It was the classic Hobbesian choice – the illusion that there is more than one choice. In fact, there was only one choice left to her: sell. Tears began streaming down her cheeks; she felt sick. She bent over and sobbed. Vincenzo just sat there waiting; he offered no words of comfort or support. It was all over.

Through her tears and sobbing, she uttered, "Yes."

Vincenzo shoved the papers and pen in front of her. "Sign here," he said coldly. With shaking hands, she sealed the transaction, and her fate. "I will contact you within the week. I will also arrange for us to travel to America." He then got up and left. Clelia was too shaken to move. She sat there staring into the void. She was completely alone now.

She had a premonition that her life was about to take an ominous turn. Every day there were more horror stories

---

[1] 1US dollar equaled 5.18 lira in 1914

about the war. Italy was now fully engaged in the conflict. People did not stray too far from home. Where there was once a vibrant nightlife, now the streets, cafes and local squares were deserted. Her mind started to wander: The convent was a safe haven, stultifying but safe. All she needed to do was pray and look after the priests and her sister nuns. Perhaps, she did make a mistake. Life was hard behind the Vatican walls, but not like this. No, there was no going back. She was no longer a "Vaticana," no longer welcome despite the simple and chaste life that she had led since leaving.

That night, sleep would not come. Despite numerous prayers and meditation, her mind was a jumble of disconnected thoughts and feelings: Vincenzo's callous treatment, the sale, the war and now the prospect of leaving Italy for a strange land. No, there would be no sleep tonight.

Chapter 20

July 31, 1914. Each day she waited for Vincenzo to return went agonizingly slowly. She was now in a state of suspended animation. She was locked into an orbit of waiting for something to happen. It would be ten days before Vincenzo returned. And when he did, the bottom fell out.

"I have the funds under lock and key for use when we arrive in America. I have booked passage on the 'Carpathia'. We will be in a first-class cabin. We depart two days from now. Be ready."

And so, it had come to this for Clelia. She was now nothing more than a mere observer in the enfolding drama. On the morning of the second day, a gruff-looking coachman came by and loaded her meagre belongings in the truck bed. "Where is Vincenzo?" she enquired.

"How should I know? I was paid to take you to the docks for the 'Carpathia,'" was his terse reply.

She sat in silence for the remainder of the journey. A mixture of fear and anxiety gripped her as the hulking 'Carpathia' came into view. Apart from the photographs of ships she had seen in her days at the tourist shop, she had never actually seen a ship before. As the truck came closer to the docking area, the ship loomed larger still. The driver stopped at the foot of the gangway, unloaded her things, and without a word, departed. Fortunately, a steward approached her and asked her if he could be of any assistance. "My name is Clelia Tessarini. I am to meet Mr. Vincenzo Talarico for passage aboard this vessel."

The steward ran his finger down the list of passengers. "Ah, yes! You are in one of our first-class suites. Allow me to accompany such an important lady." With that, he escorted her to the top deck of the ship, keeping up a constant stream of fawning comments about how fortunate he was to escort her, constantly repeating, "Such an important lady." When they reached her cabin, the steward said with a flourish, "Madame Talarico, your quarters. I wish you a bon voyage."

The instant she closed the cabin door behind her, she saw that Vincenzo was already there. His luggage and clothes were piled in a heap. There must be a mistake, she thought. Why are his things in my cabin? At that moment, Vincenzo emerged from the bathroom, clothed only in a towel. "There you are, Clelia. How do you like our accommodations? Nothing but the best for us on this historic journey."

"What have you done, Vincenzo? Why was I addressed as Madame Talarico, and where is your cabin?"

"Clelia, this is our cabin, and yes, we are traveling as man and wife. It will make our lives much easier than having to explain what is clearly forbidden."

"Clearly forbidden, on that we agree."

"To do otherwise would be to squander our money. This cabin was expensive enough."

"I will not stand for this! Not only is it wrong because we are not married, it is also a sin in the eyes of God."

For the first time, Vincenzo revealed the real person behind the mask. He grabbed her shoulders, "I don't give a damn about your social niceties or God, for that matter. This is a business deal you agreed to. Don't be so naïve!"

"If I'm naïve, then you are a fraudulent and treacherous thief. I'm leaving."

With rasping laughter, he replied, "Heh, heh. I'm afraid it's too late for that now. The ship has left the harbor. We are now officially Mr. and Mrs. Vincenzo Talarico." He then added, "This will be a four-week journey. I suggest you get used to the idea."

Chapter 21

August 1, 1914. The days passed slowly for Clelia. They seemed to meld together. She refused to leave the cabin, not even for meals or the fresh ocean air. In order to keep up the pretense of marriage, Vincenzo told the other passengers at his table that his wife was not well, suffering from seasickness. As a result, the sycophantic steward brought all her meals. With a flourish, he would flash the napkin that he offered her and set her meal before her on the elegant table. It was also the only time that she spoke and then only with a "Thank you."

The steward replied, "Your husband says that you are unwell. I do hope you are feeling a bit better." With that, he bowed and backed out the door.

Vincenzo spent less and less time in the cabin, certainly not at night. Often, several days passed that she did not see him at all. On those days that he did visit the cabin, he was drunk, smelling of stale perfume, and becoming increasingly aggressive. His rumpled and soiled clothes were a clear giveaway of his insalubrious activities. "It didn't have to be this way, Clelia." The veins in his neck were bulging, "This is your fault! No, you couldn't come down from your lofty perch to dine with me and the others. Don't forget, madame, that you are nothing but a tarted-up urchin from the Vatican with a veneer of respectability."

She reached out to smack him, but he caught her arm and pulled her into him. With a sneer, he said, "I'm going to show you what you have been missing all these years." Clelia struggled, but it was to no avail. His grip was more like a vise around her arm.

"You're hurting me; stop!"

Fueled by alcohol and anger, the look on his face was pure evil. He pushed her backward onto the bed and began ripping at her clothes. She started screaming, kicking, and lashing out at him. He punched her in the face so hard that she passed out.

She didn't remember how long she was unconscious, but found herself naked on the bed, with blood on the sheets and searing pain in her genitalia. It didn't take too long for her to realize what Vincenzo had done. She saw in the bathroom mirror what his punch did to her face. She showered, hoping that the water would wash away the horror that she had just experienced, but she could not wash away the anger and humiliation. She rolled up the bloodied sheet and sat on the bed with her knees drawn up to her chest. Who could she tell of the rape? Who would listen? After all, they were booked as a married couple. Most would look at this as a typical first-night encounter between an experienced man and a vulnerable virgin bride. Men would speak of their conquests, whereas women suffered in silence about such indignity.

At that moment, Vincenzo burst breezily into the room. His clothes were clean and pressed, and he was evidently sober. When Clelia saw him, she instinctively pulled up the coverlet to her neck and screamed at him, "You filthy animal, get out and go to hell." Vincenzo did a slight bow to maximize the *faux* gentlemen effect, "Clelia, Clelia, surely you don't mean that. We've known each other for years. I came to apologize for my behavior last evening. It was the damnable drink acting, not me. I am truly sorry for the incident. It won't happen again. I will curb my drinking from now on; you'll see the real me."

Clelia grunted and nodded, but behind her eyes, she remained unconvinced.

The following days aboard the ship were uneventful. Clelia kept to her room, having her meals delivered by the steward, Marco Bevaqua, the only person she would see on the long passage. On one occasion, Marco suggested that she might want to take a walk on the deck to take in the sun and the invigorating sea air. "I don't like the sea," she replied tersely. Later that afternoon, Vincenzo came into the stateroom to inform Clelia that this would be the last full day of the crossing. "Thank you," was all she could muster.

Late on the last morning, Vincenzo arrived at the stateroom to pack his belongings; Clelia's bags were already lined up, waiting for the steward. "Good morning, Clelia. Isn't it exciting? We are entering New York Harbour. Wouldn't you like to see the Statue of Liberty, the tall buildings and the Port of New York?" Clelia noted that he was already drunk.

"All I want is to get off this ship," she replied, "And to get away from you."

"I'm sorry that you feel that way, Clelia. I was hoping that we would put the incident behind us."

She could not contain herself and screamed, "You are an animal, Vincenzo, and a drunken one at that. I will never forget or forgive you for the indignity and humiliation of your actions."

"But, Clelia, would you abandon your new family, our investment, Felice's legacy – all for one indiscretion?" Vincenzo's patronizing tone irritated Clelia even further.

"An indiscretion, an indiscretion, you say. No, it wasn't an indiscretion. It was rape, Vincenzo, rape! If we were back in Italy, you would be in jail; here, there will be no punishment. But you will suffer damnation. The wrath of God awaits you for what you have done to me."

Just then, there was a knock at the cabin door. Marco first heard and then saw the quarreling between the couple. He walked in and quickly realized that he was standing in between the couple. Vincenzo was quick to utilize this lull to change the subject, "Marco, I will be leaving the ship first in order to make travel arrangements. Please see to it that our belongings are handled with utmost care." He nodded to Clelia and then hastily left. Marco saw Clelia's expression, "Are you all right, Mrs. Talarico?"

Clelia's response was immediate, "I am not Mrs. Talarico. My name is Miss Clelia Tessarini." Her emphasis on "Miss" told everything Marco had suspected throughout the journey.

"Yes, Miss Tessarini. Sorry. I will take the baggage to the dock and meet you there."

"Thank you, Marco. I apologize for my rudeness."

"Yes, miss, I understand."

Clelia left the room embarrassed. She silently chided herself for letting her anger spill over to the steward. Vincenzo had infected her soul.

Chapter 22

August 25, 1914. Clelia made her way through a confusing labyrinth of corridors and stairs on the ship. She realized that she would have been hopelessly lost were it not for the troop of passengers disembarking.

When she reached the bottom of the gangway onto the dock, the noise, the heat, the humidity, and the smell were overwhelming. The stevedores were oblivious to the passengers and their fancy dresses. Crates were being off-loaded amidst the curses of the dock workers. Drivers whipped their braying horses as crates, bushels, and barrels were loaded onto the carts. Clelia's stomach turned when she saw a horse being mercilessly beaten fall to its knees, trying to pull an impossibly heavy load. The driver dismounted and beat the horse more until it fell onto its side, probably dead. This was the horror that she was witnessing when she saw Vincenzo pull up with a horse-drawn cart. At the same time, Marco appeared with the luggage.

Marco alighted from the carriage to help Clelia. As he did, he heard Marco refer to Clelia as "Miss" as he loaded the luggage. Vincenzo snapped back, "I remind you to call my wife, "Mrs." You should apologize to both of us for this discourtesy."

Clelia shook her head in resignation. "Yes, sir, my apologies, sir," Marco replied. There would be no gratuity from him for his services.

Owing to Felice's prescience in forging a birth certificate for Clelia, the couple was able to clear US Immigration with no difficulty. The carriage ride took them along the Hudson River that gave Clelia magnificent views of New York Harbour on her right and the buildings on her left that were worn and dilapidated – mute testimony to the recent decline in sea trade owing to the war. Whilst Vincenzo kept up a stream of consciousness regarding his life, Clelia was awe-struck at the scenery. They turned east onto Canal Street, where for the first time, she saw squalor and poverty up close.

August weather in New York was oppressive. The heat and humidity were worse than in Rome. Combined with the sights and smells of Lower Manhattan, the ride was not for the faint of heart. The carriage turned north on lower Mulberry Street. It had been a very long hour to get this far. As the coach was closed, the heat reached levels that made it difficult for Clelia to breathe. Mulberry Street gave the lie to the notion that this was the land of opportunity where the streets "were paved with gold."

Mulberry Street was narrow, not more than carriage width. The street was so narrow that it felt to Clelia like a vise closing in on her. Throngs of people filled the streets and doorways. There were no sidewalks. People hung out windows hoping for a breeze that never came. Washing that was strung from one building to another across the street created a suffocating blanket that made breathing all the harder.

They were continuously accosted by people begging for money or for a ride to anywhere. There were buskers singing or playing violin. There were an endless number of pushcarts selling everything from fish, meat, fruits and vegetables to coal, clothing and even furniture. Then there were the ubiquitous pizza vendors hawking the "best pizza this side of Naples!"

They finally reached the corner of Mulberry and Broome streets. Vincenzo shouted to the driver, "Stop!" He leaped out of the carriage and ran to embrace his two brothers, Angelo and Domenico. The conversation was animated with arms waving and exclamations of joy when Vincenzo told them about the investment. Angelo and Domenico were standing by their pushcart that advertised Angelo's pizza and Domenico's arancini (rice balls), fresh mozzarella cheese, and a variety of Italian desserts. The pushcart business was profitable - cash only and no taxes. Vincenzo gestured to a shuttered restaurant right behind them. "I have the money to buy that place – the entire building. Forget the pushcart, let's open a restaurant with the best food on Mulberry Street and in New York City."

Clelia sat sullen and angry for nearly an hour while the three brothers exchanged stories about their lives apart. It was only when the carriage driver shouted that he wanted to leave that it drew their attention to the carriage and to its sole occupant. Vincenzo grew indignant, "You will leave when I tell you to! I will pay any extra charges," as he waved a handful of dollars at the driver to the amazement of his brothers. "Now, help the lady from the carriage," he commanded. Clelia was introduced to Angelo and Domenico. "I would like you to meet Miss Clelia Tessarini, our investment partner." Angelo and Domenico nodded courteously, "It is a pleasure, Miss Tessarini." There was no longer any need to continue the pretense of Mr. and Mrs. Talarico. Whoever this woman was did not matter one iota. The brothers had what they wanted to realize their dream. Clelia was now surplus to requirements.

He escorted her back to the carriage and handed her over to the driver. "Take her to the hotel, and be certain that her things are taken to her apartment." Turning to Clelia, he said, "I'll be along shortly." He turned and left her to the driver. Her shock and anger over the past weeks had now mutated into hatred. She realized this was his plan all along. She was merely an expendable pawn, the cash point in his plan. There was no feeling for her whatsoever; even the basic courtesies had disappeared.

It was four days later when Vincenzo went to the hotel. Clelia had been abandoned, sitting alone in her room. She only left to have a sparse meal in the dining room. She spoke to no one and saw no one during those four days. Vincenzo, in the meanwhile, was celebrating his reunification with Angelo and Domenico and a successful albeit over-priced offer and acceptance for the building. No matter, the only person who was out the money was Clelia.

Chapter 23

August 31, 1914. Within four days of their initial meeting, the brothers had successfully closed a deal for the purchase of the building. Refurbishment would be costly, but there was still enough cash to accomplish their goal of making "Domenico's" restaurant a landmark dining place for the next one hundred and ten years.

Clelia's stomach churned when she realized that she had missed her monthly period. She reasoned that the trauma aboard the ship, coupled with the extended traveling, could be the reason; at least, she hoped that was the case. But what if it were true that she was pregnant? She thought about what Felice might say if he heard this news. The feelings of shame and disgust came over her. She decided to wait for another month to be certain.

Before she was able to think any further, Vincenzo burst into the room, giddy as a schoolboy. "Congratulations, Clelia, we are the owners of the building and the restaurant. It wouldn't have happened without your generosity. Thank you, thank you. Once the remodeling is complete, we will have a grand opening. Isn't that wonderful?"

She nodded but said nothing about the possible pregnancy. "Will we be living in the building?" she inquired.

"Of course, my dear. We will occupy the top floor apartment."

"When will it be ready?"

"I expect that it will be at least another month before the restaurant and our apartments are ready."

"And I presume that I will be living in this room alone for the next month?"

Vincenzo felt the sting of her comment, but went on, "I am afraid so, my dear Clelia. I will be here as often as I can but you understand that there is much to do. You must be strong."

Vincenzo then made a flourishing bow, "Thank you, again, Clelia. I must go." With that, he turned and left the room.

She was angry with herself. Why didn't she insist on getting more involved? After all, it was her money. No, it was Felice's, but she should have demanded a say. In fact, she knew more about running a restaurant business from the kitchen to the dining room than the three of them combined. And she could cook better than the brothers. But now, she had allowed herself to become just an observer or even an interloper.

She spent the rest of the day alternatively reading the news and the Bible. She had so many conflicting emotions, the primary among them was the possibility of a pregnancy. She had lost her appetite after Vincenzo's visit. Clelia said her prayers and turned out the light. It was going to be a long month.

Chapter 24

September 30, 1914. Each day passed agonizingly slow. Clelia fought the constant feeling of being trapped and isolated. Vincenzo was now in complete control of her life. She had no money of her own; she had no idea what Vincenzo was doing with it. She was likely pregnant, an unmarried woman alone in a large city; she could not speak English. She had come to the realization that she had become expendable. These feelings paled as she realized that she had missed her second monthly period.

The awareness that she was now pregnant pressed on her chest. She had to tell Vincenzo but was afraid of his reaction, particularly when he was drunk. She was witness to his aggression; he could fly into a rage whenever the news or facts did not suit him. She was the victim of a rape perpetrated by Vincenzo; it was also his baby. He had to know that she was a virgin at the time, so there was no possibility of any other sexual encounter. The thought that he would deny the rape and pregnancy was too much for her to contemplate. There would be no consideration whatsoever for an abortion.

One morning, shortly after breakfast, she suddenly became nauseous. This would be the first of many episodes of morning sickness. After collecting herself, she went to lie on the bed. She pulled up her knees to her chest and cried herself to sleep. By the time she awoke, the afternoon sun was casting long shadows. At that moment, Vincenzo burst into the room. There were no courtesies, just a curt, "Why are you in bed?" And there it was; the opening she needed.

With tears in her eyes, she shouted, "Because I'm pregnant, Vincenzo, pregnant with your baby. See what you have done!" Vincenzo was shocked. Thoughts came to him in flashes: *what does this mean for me; what does it mean for our venture? What would the brothers think?*

"Are you certain?" came the patronizing reply. "It could be fatigue from your journey, the heat and humidity, and the stress of recent events."

"No, there is no mistake, I am pregnant with your baby."

Vincenzo's tone and demeanor changed at the words, "your baby." He was visibly shaken, "What are we going to do, Clelia?"

Clelia's reaction surprised him: "You will first open a bank account in my name with sufficient funds for our baby; you will contact the local nurse for a visit, and you will ensure that our apartment is completed before any other. After that, I don't care what you do."

Vincenzo left as abruptly as he came. This development changed his grand plan, which now had to include a sham marriage and his dream of living the life of the gay entrepreneur together with his two siblings.

Installed in a commodious flat, Clelia could take care of herself and her baby. Now he needed time to think. He went to the local pub, poured down several whiskeys, and went through nearly a pack of Italian cigars. He had to tell his brothers not that he raped her but that the sex was consensual. Knowing his brothers, an admission of rape would not be well received. So, that was step one. The next step would be to marry Clelia. It wasn't any sense of chivalry that motivated him. He knew all too well that it was the "decent thing" to do in such a case, but decency was not a part of his modus operandi. Marriage was the expedient thing to do. Under no circumstances was anyone to know that the marriage was one of convenience, a marriage that would not be one of love, but the means to cover his indiscretion. He concluded that it wasn't the rape itself that concerned him; he had committed similar offenses on other reluctant women before. What disturbed him most of all was the effect the knowledge of rape would have on the local Italian community – his potential customers and, as a result, on their start-up business.

Chapter 25

Later that evening, Vincenzo went to the newly purchased building on Mulberry Street. The renovation was underway as painters scrambled up and down the scaffolding. Table and chairs were piled high in a corner. Kitchen equipment had already been installed under the scrutiny of the newly appointed chef and was ready for the first customer.

Walking carefully around and over the detritus, paint buckets and toolboxes, Vincenzo went to his brothers to inform his brothers about Clelia. "Hello, my dear brothers.

I see that we are making speedy progress. Are the apartments ready?"

"Almost, Vincenzo, what is the hurry?" replied Domenico.

"I intend to marry Miss Tessarini, and would like to relocate her from the hotel, which is costing us too much money, money that we need to launch this business."

I would also like your blessings.

Domenico spoke first, "Well, that is both surprising and good news, Vincenzo." Of the three brothers, Domenico was both the most intelligent and world-wise. He was also very perceptive. He suspected that there was another shoe to drop. Vincenzo was sweating and his face was flushed.

Domenico continued, "Is there anything else, Vincenzo, something else that we should know about Miss Tessarini?"

Vincenzo hoped that the marriage announcement would be the end of the matter. Domenico continued to look deeply into Vincenzo's eyes. It was no use, "Clelia is pregnant."

"May I presume that it was consensual?" Domenico's tone had changed.

"Yes," Vincenzo lied.

Domenico was not entirely convinced. He knew his brother all too well. There was more to this story, but he decided not to pursue it any further lest it have repercussions on their relationship as brothers and equally on the business. The woman was pregnant. How she got pregnant was no longer an issue. Angelo had said nothing, but the eye-to-eye communication between Domenico and him also told him that there were more unspoken aspects to this story.

Angelo spoke for both, "You have our blessings, dear Vincenzo. Is there anything that she needs to make her comfortable during her time?"

"As a matter of fact, there is, Angelo. I don't know any doctors. I think it would be helpful if a doctor or nurse monitored her progress."

Domenico spoke, "I know a very good doctor. I will arrange it."

Chapter 26

October 10, 1914. When Clelia answered the knock at her door, she was surprised to see a man and a woman standing, one carrying a black bag. "Good morning. Are you Miss Clelia Tessarini?" the woman enquired.

Unaccustomed to visitors, her initial reaction was fear. *Who are these people? What do they want?* "Yes, I am Clelia Tessarini," she replied cautiously.

"I am Doctor Frangella, and this is my nurse, Miss Bartolo. Mr. Domenico Talarico asked us to come by. We are here to offer any medical care or advice in the light of your pregnancy. May we come in?"

Clelia was surprised, but welcomed the attention. "Yes, of course, please come in."

The doctor explained that with her permission, they would examine her and prescribe any medication, if needed, to help her through her pregnancy. The nurse was there to assist the doctor and reassure Clelia during the examination. After explaining the examination procedure, he asked, "Are you ready to proceed? This will be uncomfortable, but I assure you that this is standard procedure."

Clelia was suddenly frightened at the prospect of a male doctor conducting an examination, particularly in light of recent events aboard the ship. Seeing the expression on her face, the nurse reached out and held Clelia's hand, "It will be all right. I'll be right here."

Nurse Bartolo assisted Clelia with removing some of her clothes and putting on a dressing gown. Absent an examining table, Clelia would have to lie in bed for the examination. As she did so, all the fear and anger from the rape came rushing forward. "Please, doctor, I don't know if I can do this."

"It is your choice, my dear. We can return when you are further along."

Dr. Frangella stood up, prepared to leave. She took a deep breath and with tears in her eyes, she blurted, "I am afraid, doctor. I am afraid of men."

With that comment, the doctor understood her fear and anxiety, and probably the true cause of that trepidation. "Of course, I understand. I will not force you, but may I suggest that an examination at this stage will give us a clear picture of your pregnancy and reassure you that all is well with your baby."

Clelia sat at the edge of the bed with tears streaming down her cheeks. The rocking motion helped to calm her as she came to grips with the procedure. Yes, she knew that it was the right thing to do, but first, she had to address the gut-wrenching feelings of vulnerability, Vincenzo, the sale of the restaurant, the awful trip, and her current isolation. And yet, she had to confront the reality that she would soon be a mother with an obligation to an unborn child. The doctor and the nurse were here to help. She took a deep breath, "Very well, doctor, you are quite right, of course. I am ready." The last words came out hesitatingly.

Nurse Bartolo helped Clelia onto the bed and propped her head with pillows. She held her hand and then nodded to the doctor to proceed. Midway through the procedure, Doctor Frangella stopped and looked both angry and sad, "You were raped, weren't you?"

"Yes," was all she could reply.

Within a matter of moments, the doctor had completed his examination. "I have checked the fetal heartbeat. I am pleased to report that you and your baby are well. It is a normal pregnancy."

"Thank you, doctor, thank you. I am sorry that I caused such a fuss."

"Clelia, Nurse Bartolo will give you nutrition information. You and your baby need fresh air and good food. I will see you in two months. In the meantime, look after yourself."

Clelia offered to pay the doctor and the nurse for their services. Doctor Frangella replied, "It is not necessary. Mr. Domenico Talarico has generously covered the fee."

With that, both doctor and nurse left Clelia to her thoughts. Seeing the doctor and the nurse, the examination, and revealing that she was raped seemed to help in a small way. It was a temporary respite from the feelings of anger and humiliation.

Chapter 27

December 21, 1914. Taking her doctor's advice, Clelia ended her self-enforced isolation to take a walk along Mulberry Street. The sun was shining down the cavernous streets as she inhaled the crisp winter air that made her nose run. Christmas was just four days away; the streets were already festooned with flags and lights. It was the first time since leaving Rome that she allowed herself the sensations of Christmas, the chill in the air, and the smell of food cooking. Under different circumstances, she might have allowed herself to feel happy. She peered into the shops to marvel at the Christmas decorations and goods on sale. Further down the street, she saw the Church of the Precious Blood, the gathering spot for the newly arrived Italian immigrants.

The Church was empty but still had the feint fragrance of incense from an earlier service. She took the last pew. Unlike the silence of her room, this silence she told herself was the presence of God. It was a momentary respite from the misery she had experienced recently. She said her daily rosary and, while doing so, allowed her mind to wander back to her days in the Vatican. Despite being a strict and oppressive environment, it was at the same time tranquil and comforting. What would it have been like if she had remained and become a nun? Surely, her life would have been different; but she would not have experienced the joy of her papa, Felice. There would be no restaurant, no travel agency, and most assuredly, no Vincenzo. She lit a candle and continued to sit, enjoying the serenity of the moment.

Meanwhile, a little bit further up Mulberry Street, Angelo, Domenico and Vincenzo were meeting to discuss progress on the renovations on the floors above the restaurant. Angelo was displeased at the pace of the restoration of the three apartments. He had summoned the contractor and threatened to cancel the contract if the work was not completed as agreed. As a long-time resident of Mulberry Street, his pushcart had become a fixture in this close-knit community and known for his authentic pizzas. Any attempts by the contractor at retribution for canceling the contract would be met with swift and painful street justice.

The new restaurant, "Domenico's," was opened with musical and theatrical fanfare, blessings from the Church, and publicity from the local Italian newspaper. It immediately started doing a brisk business. The clientele were mostly resident Italians wanting a taste of the old country. The brothers divided the business to maximize their individual talents. Angelo was responsible for the kitchen and the menu. Domenico managed the business, purchasing, and the staff with the occasional tour of the restaurant floor for people to see the person behind the sign on the door. Vincenzo did what he had always done as the "front of house" – mingling with the diners, buying drinks for particular customers, and consuming copious quantities of wine in the process, followed by a late-night whiskey – or two. He had found his voice and his calling; he was the *maître di* of Domenico's. He found that he also had a reasonably pleasant singing voice. On several occasions during the evening, accompanied by an accordionist, he would break out into Neapolitan songs and encourage the diners to join in.

Clelia left the Church to make her way back to the hotel. After sitting in the Church, she felt that she had put the anger and hatred aside momentarily to enjoy the day. It was already twilight when she walked onto the street; the short December days, together with the frosty air, were accompanied by snowfall, the first she had ever experienced. Much like a child, she giggled as she stuck her tongue out to taste the snow.

Back in her room, she was surrounded by the isolation and the silence; it was suffocating. The only sound was made by the trucks and people getting an early start on Christmas celebrations. Despite the gloom from her surroundings, Clelia was becoming more accustomed to her pregnancy. She could not allow her anger and guilt to affect the child inside her. She got on her knees to make a vow that she would suppress those feelings and find the special joy of motherhood.

Chapter 28

The months dragged on for Clelia, broken only by the occasional walk along Mulberry Street and a visit to the Church. Each day was a challenge confronting her demons. The monotony was also periodically interrupted by the visits by Dr. Frangella and Nurse Bartolo to conduct the increasing number of examinations. The doctor assured Clelia that all was well with both her and her child.

After one such visit, the doctor enquired, "Have you given any thought to names for your baby – boy or girl?"

"Yes, doctor, I have." Clelia had selected the names early on. "If the baby is a boy, then his name will be Felice; if a girl, then Felicia – in honor of my father."

"Those are lovely names, Clelia. The examination tells me that your time is coming very soon. I will be here every two weeks from here on. Be certain to eat; and keep up your daily walks."

After both doctor and nurse left, Clelia got to her knees at the bedside to thank God for a healthy child. No sooner that she had finished her prayers that Vincenzo came bursting into the room.

"I have wonderful news, Clelia. Our apartment is ready!"

"Yes, that is good news," she said flatly. "Just in time for our baby. Clelia would not let the moment pass without reminding him of his perfidy.

"I will make arrangements for us to move into the flat within the next two weeks," Vincenzo replied, purposefully avoiding her comment regarding "our baby".

"You are going to be pleased with your new home. Your wait is almost over. I must leave, Clelia." And as quickly as he came, he turned and left. He was in a hurry to get back to the restaurant, fortify himself with a few whiskeys, and meet the first guests for the evening.

When he arrived at the restaurant, he found both stern-faced brothers waiting for him. Angelo enquired, "Vincenzo, have you been to see that poor woman of yours? She has been alone for too long. We must arrange for your marriage immediately. I have already spoken with the priest who will perform the ceremony. Do you understand, Vincenzo?"

As Vincenzo reached for the bottle of whiskey, Domenico asked again, "Do you understand, Vincenzo? May we presume that you have been keeping up your payments for her medical care?"

"Yes, I understand," he said indignantly, and for emphasis, added, "Yes, I understand. Will that be all? I have quests to greet in a few minutes."

"No, Vincenzo, I don't think you entirely understand what is about to happen. This is not just about the birth of any child. This child will be a member of our family. We – you – will be assuming an enormous responsibility. Moreover, he or she will inherit our business. How many times have you visited with her, spoken to her, and given some indication that you care about her welfare? We know that this child was an accident on your part, but accident or not, you need to face that obligation. And, your brother and I don't think that you have."

Vincenzo was furious at being treated like an adolescent. "I will not be spoken to in this manner. You both forget that it was I who brought you the money to invest. If not I, then you would both be struggling with your pushcart business selling pizzas." He reached for the whiskey bottle and took several mouthfuls directly from it in a show of his defiance. "I have to see to the guests."

Chapter 29

May 11, 1915. Clelia did not sleep the entire night. The pains from the contractions were excruciating. She struggled to get out of bed to say her prayers, and as she did so, her waters broke. She called for a bellman to take a message to Doctor Frangella that she was having close contractions and that her waters had broken. The terrified bellman nearly fell over a chair as he rushed from the room. Within a few minutes, both doctor and nurse rushed into her room. Clelia was lying on the floor curled up, gasping for breath and trying hard not to scream.

"We're here, Clelia. Let's get you onto the bed. You are about to have a baby!"

Unfortunately, Dr. Frangella's attempt at levity was lost on Clelia. Her contractions were coming faster and faster even as the pain was increasing. The most difficult part was about to begin: the hard labor. With encouraging words like "bear down", "push," and "you are doing so well", Clelia delivered her baby nearly six hours after her labor began.

"It's a boy, Clelia. You have a healthy baby boy. Congratulations!"

Clelia started to apologize for crying throughout her labor, and toward the end, screaming, but the nurse dismissed it as part of the process of childbirth. "Do not concern yourself. You did so well."

Clelia was exhausted from the ordeal, but for the moment, forgot as the nurse laid the baby on her chest. She whispered, "Hello, Felice. I'm Clelia, your mother." She then drifted off to sleep. She awoke with a fright. How long was I asleep? Where is my baby?

Nurse Bartolo read Clelia's thoughts, "You have been asleep for four hours. I have bathed baby Felice and wrapped him in blankets. Dr. Frangella had another emergency to attend to."

Clelia took baby Felice, who was sleeping quietly. "Thank you, thank you so much for all that you have done for me. However, can I repay you?"

Nurse Bartolo smiled and responded gently, "Having a healthy child is repayment enough. Besides, Vincenzo Talarico and his brothers have paid handsomely."

"There is so much to do, and I am alone without family."

Nurse Bartolo assured her patient, "You are not alone, Clelia. Do not worry. Rest now. I will see to everything you need. I will leave you now for several hours as I need to organize a baptism for the baby, and purchase baby clothes and food."

It was early evening by the time the nurse returned together with an out-of-breath hotel bellman carrying so many bundles that he needed to peer around them to find his way into the room. Clelia woke up with a start. "It is only me," the nurse responded, "and this clod who complains of back strain."

For the first time since Rome, Clelia laughed, really laughed. She thanked the bellman, who was just so happy to retreat from the domineering Nurse Bartolo. Clelia propped herself up on the bed whilst Nurse Bartolo piled the numerous bags and boxes on the bed.

"This is like the Christmas I remember with my papa." Clelia had forgotten the pain, the agony of the previous weeks, and all her troubles, including Vincenzo, …for the moment.

Nurse Bartolo laughed, "Christmas perhaps, but wait until baby Felice wakes up crying in the middle of the night and requires feeding and changing."

But Clelia was too overwhelmed with unpacking to hear Nurse Barolo. Indeed, for Clelia, at least, it was Christmas.

Chapter 30

May 18, 1915. Baby Felice was baptized at the Church of the Precious Blood on Lower Mulberry Street. Domenico was the sponsor, together with Nurse Bartolo. Angelo and a sullen-looking Vincenzo stood by to respond to prayers. The simple ceremony lasted only several minutes, after which the party went to their restaurant for a celebration. Angelo was the first to speak, "Clelia, today you and Felice become a part of the Talarico family. We are proud and grateful to you for bringing this beautiful child into the world." Domenico echoed the sentiment. Vincenzo nodded his head, "Thank you," the first words that he had spoken all afternoon. He was clearly still chaffing over his encounter with his brothers. During dinner, Angelo was in an animated conversation with Nurse Bartolo. Domenico spent most of the dinner engaged with Clelia asking questions about her life and the Restaurant in Rome. Clelia was thrilled with the attention she so desperately craved. Domenico listened attentively, never taking his eyes off her. The gaze was warm and sincere. Apart from her conversations with the nurse and the doctor, no one had spoken with her regarding her previous life. Indeed, she had had very few human interactions since her arrival. During those moments, she dared to think that happiness was achievable. By the end of the dinner, the reality of her new life snuffed out any hope of happiness: Vincenzo was so intoxicated that he stumbled over his chair. Neither of the brothers offered to help.

After dinner, Domenico invited Clelia to see her new home. The size of the flat, the furniture, and the kitchen were breathtaking. She had never seen such spacious and luxurious accommodations. She smiled, "Thank you, Domenico, for all you have done for me and Felice."

"Clelia, you are now a member of our family with a very important part to play. You and Felice deserve our love and support. Of this, I promise you," Domenico said solemnly.

But the special moment was broken when a very drunk Vincenzo barged into the room.

"See my dear Clelia, what I have done for us and for Felice," he slurred as he steadied himself against a wall. "Did I not promise this? Did not our investment prove to be a good one?"

Domenico had heard enough. "Be quiet, Vincenzo. I have since learned from Clelia that it is she who provided all the funds for this investment. We owe her a debt of gratitude. You have embarrassed yourself again. Go to the guest bedroom and sleep it off."

Vincenzo was furious and becoming increasingly belligerent. "No, it is I that deserves the gratitude. It is I that convinced her to invest. It is I who organized for her to come to this country. And it is I who took both you and Angelo off the streets from behind a pushcart and into this restaurant."

Domenico, who was a large framed man, and at least one and half times the weight of his brother, walked over to Vincenzo with fists balled. Vincenzo backed away, but in doing so, he slumped over backward, vomiting on his way down.

"Clelia, I am so sorry about this. You don't deserve him. Help me get him into bed. I don't know where else I could take him," Domenico shook his head. Although he did not confide it to Clelia, he had a premonition that this would end badly for everyone.

Chapter 31

July 15, 1916. The summer heat was oppressive, especially in a third-floor walk-up. Opening windows did little to provide relief. The heat and smell from the street below wafted into her apartment. She thought that a walk might help her and Felice to cool down. Armed with her parasol, Clelia entered Mulberry Street with Felice sitting happily in a pushchair, a gift from Angelo and Domenico. She was struck by a blast of heat as she opened the door. What struck her more than the heat was the rancid smell of rotting food, horse shit and sewage. Mulberry Street was narrow – more like a large path between buildings. Here people, animals, pushcarts and horse-drawn taxis all vied for a space. The sidewalk was so narrow that making progress consisted of one foot at a time, accompanied by a constant "Pardon me" as she negotiated the street. She managed to reach the church where she thought she would say her daily rosary. The interior was decidedly cooler than the street, and quiet. She settled into one of the pews and began her prayers. The cool air was a welcome relief. Felice had fallen peacefully asleep, allowing her to sit peacefully to contemplate her life's condition. She asked only for peace for her and Felice. Her reverie was broken by the sound of the voices in the vestibule. How long had she been there? She turned to see Felice sitting happily, playing with a toy. She did love him but only from a distance. He was the sole reason for her existence, for better and for worse. She committed to remain with him for the rest of her life. The least she could do was to shield him from dangers, real or perceived.

This was the lens through which she viewed her life: danger. She was alone, angry and without a real family or friends except for Nurse Bartolo. Although she was grateful to the two brothers for helping her, she still felt that it was only by sufferance that she continued to live in the apartment that she knew was really meant for Vincenzo.

It was late afternoon when Clelia made her way back to the apartment. The street was so crowded that people began walking, only turning aside to make way for a carriage accompanied by shouts of the driver to "get out of the way!" Her apartment was just as hot as when she left it. She peeled off her clothes, leaving on just enough to preserve her sense of modesty.

Just as she settled in, there was a knock at the door. She hastily donned a dressing gown. She opened the door to find Angelo and Domenico standing in front of her.

"May we come in?" Angelo asked.

"Sorry, yes, of course. Do come in."

"Have you seen Vincenzo? We are worried about his safety."

Seeing the expression on Clelia's face, Domenico offered, "I know that things between him and you are not good. He has not been in the restaurant for a week. That is unlike him. Knowing him as you do, do you have any idea where he might be? We would be grateful for any information."

At first, she thought she would say, "I know where he is; he is in Hell where he belongs." But she demurred. Mindful that they were still brothers, she thought as a matter of courtesy, she would offer her thoughts. "I am not certain, but you may want to try the hotel where I stayed. If not there, then I would suggest that the house of ill-repute on Grand Street. I know that he has frequented that place."

The remark stung both brothers, who glanced at each other. It was the one place that they thought he would not visit as he already had enough women friends whom he might pursue. "Thank you, Clelia. As sad as that sounds, we are grateful for your courtesy," said Angelo as she shook his head.

Domenico looked at Felice crawling around on the carpet. He smiled. "We have a beautiful member of our family." Domenico leaned over, picked up the child, and held it to his chest. Felice looked puzzled, but accepted the hug – something he rarely felt. "Yes, a beautiful child."

"How have you been, Clelia?" Domenico continued. It was clear to Clelia that Domenico was being sincere.

"Aside from my fear of Vincenzo, my life has settled down to the day-to-day monotony of caring for a baby."

Always the gentleman, Domenico enquired, "Is there anything you need or want? You need but ask."

Clelia was quick to respond, "There is something. Not since the baptism have I been in the restaurant. I would be delighted if we could have dinner together."

Both brothers were surprised by her frankness. "Of course, Clelia, of course! Would you be available for dinner this evening?"

"Yes, that would be nice." For the first time in recent memory, she smiled.

"Then it is settled," Domenico added. "I will collect you at 7:00 o'clock for dinner with Angelo and me. I look forward to it." With that, both brothers excused themselves. Clelia was pleased with the outcome of this encounter, a first for her, but she couldn't help be skeptical of their motives. Why, after so long, had they waited to offer an invitation? Especially since she had provided the investment money and, more importantly, Felice, their nephew, a new member of the family.

Dinner was an extravagant affair: an individual waiter for each of the three diners, the finest Italian wine, and course after course, followed by a serenade from one of the featured sopranos at the Metropolitan Opera. Clelia was the center of attention, and had to admit to herself that she was loving every moment of it. Her eyes sparkled and her cheeks flushed. She felt like she had all those years ago with her papa. It had been so long since anyone had taken any interest in her, in her life with all its tragedies and broken dreams. Vincenzo was not mentioned. The questions came fast: tell us about your papa, Clelia; tell us about the restaurant, what was on the menu; the number of tables, the type of guests. Her answers clearly indicated that she had more than just a passing knowledge of the restaurant business. Angelo had been scribbling notes on a napkin. Domenico was particularly interested in her earlier days in the Vatican; her testimony at the canonical hearing to consider sainthood for Pope Pius IX; the intrigue surrounding his papacy, and the machinations of the Church caught up in the violence and unrest.

Dinner concluded with Limoncello and gentlemanly bows from both brothers. They had to admit that it was a worthwhile dinner.

"Clelia, Angelo and I are so pleased that we had this opportunity to get to know you better. I shall accompany you to your apartment," Domenico said as he pointed to the door

Chapter 32

February 14, 1917. The United States was now fully committed to the war in Europe. The call for manpower was greeted with enthusiasm and rampant displays of patriotism. Spectators gathered as the American troops, the "doughboys", marched down Broadway accompanied by rousing martial music: "It's a Long, Long Way to Tipperary," "How Are You Going to Keep Them Down on the Farm," and "Tell That to the Marines". Patriotic posters festooned every available wall calling on young men to sign up to fight.

It was a short walk to Lower Broadway. Clelia found a spot for her and Felice, who was seated in a pram and wrapped tightly to fend off the bitter cold of February. She marveled at the crowds waving and singing as the troops came marching by. She wondered whether there were any Italian boys in the mix; she concluded probably not, given Italy's initial support for Germany, later switching sides. She enjoyed the pageantry, the music and the encouraging shouts from the crowd. There were the ubiquitous pushcarts hawking everything from hot coffee spiked with anisette, cold pizza, ice cream, sweet and savory treats and cakes. Clelia indulged herself and had the coffee-anisette brew. The warmth felt good in her throat. By this time, however, she could feel the biting cold on her feet and hands. "Let's go, Felice. If we stay any longer, we will most certainly freeze to death." She just managed to get to the front door of the building when it started to snow. It lasted for two days without let up, leaving streets impassable for both man and beast. The city had ground to a halt.

She sat by her window overlooking Mulberry Street as residents and shopkeepers shoveled the sidewalks, but threw the snow into the street. The mounds were so high that the street became an impromptu playground for children and their sleds. The restaurant stayed open for the occasional guests who were brave enough to navigate the mountains of snow.

The last afternoon light cast grotesque shadows from buildings onto the now silent snowy streets. Clelia stared into the distance, not thinking anything really. She drew the curtains, turned to Felice and said, "I imagine that you must be hungry. Tonight, I shall prepare something simple and warm: pasta with anchovy sauce."

Later that evening, after putting Felice to bed, she said her prayers, got into bed, and turned out the light. In the darkness, she let her mind wander back to Rome, the restaurant, the good times and her papa. She wondered what it was like in the Eternal City. So much had changed in her life; she was so far from her starting point. Now with a child depending on her, she had no idea of the end point. Was this place to be that end point? Something told her that there were a few more chapters to be read in her life story.

Chapter 33

May 11, 1917. Felice was two years old today. He was now walking and talking. It took Clelia's breath away chasing after him lest he fall or worse, climb on to the table or climb in the bathtub. But it was also a day that Clelia struggled to find happiness in this event. Her little boy was growing up. The winter months were now just a memory; it was Spring, a sunny day on this Friday, May 11th.

Clelia felt the crisp air as she walked along Mulberry Street on her way to church together with Felice. They entered the church just as a mass was being said – perfect timing for her. At the conclusion of the service, Clelia met the parish priest, Father Joseph Variale, who listened to her confessions, and lately had become her spiritual advisor and confidant. She struggled with anger and rage at the man who lied to her, raped her, and otherwise made her life a misery – all except for Felice. Father Variale, a mild-mannered Franciscan Friar, listened intently, and then offered, "My child, we can neither change the past nor correct the sins of an evil man. This is your cross to bear, but you are not alone. Christ is with you; the church is with you, and I am with you. I know that Nurse Bartolo has been your friend for these many months. Oh, and by the way, please tell Nurse Bartolo that I haven't seen her at mass for two weeks."

Clelia offered a weak smile and offered, "Thank you, Father. I will tell her."

The priest placed his hands on Felice's and her head and blessed both. He then gave Felice a kiss on his forehead. "Go with God in peace, Clelia, you have my blessing."

"Thank you, Father," she responded. She genuflected at the altar, turned and left. From the silence and dimness of the church, she met the blazing sun along with the clamor in the streets. She shielded her eyes and tried unsuccessfully to blot out the noise. But this was life on Mulberry Street. There was no escaping the cacophony. She made her way back to the apartment, fed Felice, and sat in a chair to reflect on Friar Variale's kind words. She fell into a fitful sleep that ended with another bad dream featuring Vincenzo. She awoke with her arms flailing to ward off his blows. "When will this end? When will I be free of this living nightmare?" Her thoughts were interrupted by Felice who was pulling at her skirt. "Mama, I'm hungry."

Chapter 34

April 18, 1918. It had been an uneventful year thus far. The Christmas holidays came and went. Felice received several toys from his two uncles. Vincenzo was nowhere to be seen. It was as if he disappeared off the face of the earth. Clelia took that to be a good sign.

The day began as most of her days did over the past three years. She said her morning prayers, fed Felice, and did her morning housework. It had been a week of heavy downpours, thunder and lightning. She and Felice had been confined to looking at the flooding street below. The rain had not let up for the entire day. Darkness descended quickly; house lights were on throughout the city.

Clelia and Felice had just finished dinner when there was a loud banging on her door. It wasn't a knock, but an urgent demand. And she heard a voice that made her shudder: Vincenzo!

"Open this damned door! I want to see my son." His speech was slurred, his tone menacing. "Open the door I said. You are my wife; you must do what I say. I have a right to see my son."

At hearing his voice, the memories from years of abuse came flooding back. She felt the same cold chill as in the past. Her chest felt like a weight had descended on her. She took in large gulps of air as she backed away from the door. From somewhere deep inside her, she wanted him dead, out of Felice's and her lives for good. She screamed, "You will never see my son; you will only come in here over my dead body. Go back to the gutter you came from."

Vincenzo had kept hammering on the door without letting up, screaming curses and threats. Suddenly, however, it stopped. She could hear his heavy footfalls as he descended or rather, stumbled his way down the stairs. Hearing the banging and raised voices, Felice had begun to cry. She rushed over to him and held him for a long time. "My dear, dear Felice, it's all right. No one is going to hurt us. Never fear, my son, for as long as I live, you will always be by my side." Just then, she heard a clap of thunder. "Come, let us look at the pouring rain, and watch the people on the street below scurrying with their useless umbrellas."

Holding Felice, she stared out the window listening to the thunder and watching flashes of lightning flash across the sky.

Suddenly, like a ghostly apparition, Vincenzo's face appeared in the window. She screamed and took several steps back. Despite being so inebriated, Vincenzo managed to climb the fire escape to their third-floor apartment. His face was contorted, more like a terrifying ghoulish mask. Despite the pouring rain, Vincenzo could see Felice in Clelia's arms. He called out, "Felice, my son, I am your papa."

Although terrified, she screamed, "He is not your son; he is my son. You lost your right to fatherhood a long time ago."

He snarled, "You whore, I will have my son, and then I will kill you for what you have done to me."

He was about to break in through the window. He staggered back, preparing to kick, but had miscalculated the distance to the railing and the slippery footing. He stumbled backward, and in an instant, was gone. Immediately, there were screams from the street below. Within minutes, the scream of police sirens punctured the night. Clelia stood frozen in her spot. It all happened so fast; it seemed somehow surreal.

Vincenzo lay in a pool of water in a twisted and contorted position, surrounded by police and curious onlookers. The commotion outside the restaurant brought several diners to the street as well as Angelo and Domenico. Upon seeing his dead brother, Domenico dropped to his knees, shaking his head. "What have you done, dear brother? What have you done?

Angelo looked up, and in an instant, knew what had happened. He turned away from the gruesome scene and ran into the building, taking two steps at a time. When he got to the third floor, Clelia was standing at the open door.

Angelo's voice was hoarse and hard, "Woman, what have you done? You killed our brother, your husband."

Clelia was distraught; she felt that in some way, she was responsible for the death of a human being. True, he was a vile and dangerous man, but still a man who did not deserve to die from a fall from a slippery fire escape. What a senseless and useless way to die! She looked at Angelo, hoping against hope that Vincenzo may have survived the fall, but she knew better. A part of her was glad that he was finally out of her life. She hated him but the realization that she played an unwitting part in his death brought the bile up to her throat.

"I…I tried to keep him from the door. He was in a fierce state, threatening to take Felice and then kill me. I couldn't let him in. It never occurred to me that he would climb the fire escape. I saw him in the window, his teeth were barred, his expression was vicious and terrifying. He stepped back to kick it open. As he did so, he slipped and disappeared over the railing. I didn't know that he was dead; I was so afraid to go out for fear he would take Felice and do harm to me. Please, Angelo, you must believe me; I meant him no harm. I just wanted him to stay away."

"Was his death the only solution to keeping him away? Did you try to reason with him? Did you try to call us to intervene? If you had, this would never have happened. Come downstairs outside. I want you to see what you have done."

Now in the street, she could see his lifeless, twisted body soaked in the rain. The usually dapper man looked more like a rag doll. When she saw blood trickling from his ear and nose, she fainted.

She awoke with a start. *Felice? Where is Felice?* She then felt the warm hand and reassuring voice of Nurse Bartolo. "It's all right, Clelia, you and Felice are quite safe. You need to rest; it has been a dreadful night. Here, I have made you some tea."

She found herself sitting in her bed, undressed from her wet street clothes to her night dress – Nurse Bartolo's doing. "How did you know?" she asked.

"One of Vincenzo's brothers called me and told me all of what happened," she replied. "Vincenzo's body has been moved to the morgue. I imagine the police will want to speak to you. You have not been accused of any wrongdoing. So, there is no need to worry. Now rest, I will stay with you tonight."

Chapter 35

April 19, 1918. The police did come to take Clelia's statement. They concluded that Vincenzo's death was an unfortunate accident. For Clelia, that was the end of a tragic, ill-fated episode in her life. She needed to give herself a fresh start with the same enthusiasm that she had earlier in her life in Italy, in the travel agency and in Felice's restaurant.

It was a crisp spring day with the sun cascading between the buildings on Mulberry Street. She threw open the window overlooking the street, and winced momentarily at the fire escape. No, she would not allow herself such maudlin and depressing thoughts. What's done is done. Today was the first day in her new life. Just as she began her daily cleaning ritual, there was a knock at the door. It was Angelo.

"May I come in?"

Strange, she thought, no morning greeting, just a business-like air. "Yes, of course, Angelo," she said brightly.

"I have come on a matter of grave importance. We saw the police report exonerating you of any responsibility. That is the official ruling. Unofficially, we are not quite as sanguine. I, we, think that this tragedy would not have occurred if you had called us. We would not have let him in your apartment, but we would have restrained him. It is because of this we are unable to forgive you. As a result, we are asking you to leave here. Besides, a single woman with a child living in this building would not be seen well in our community or in our business."

Clelia was stunned as she listened. Tears welled up in her eyes as she tried to comprehend the enormity of the situation. "Please, Angelo, try to understand. If I did let him in, he would have killed me. There was no time to call you. He was blocking the doorway. Would you have preferred a murder in this building and a child kidnapping by a drunken man?"

"The child's father," he interrupted.

"Yes, his father. Would you have preferred to see me dead, and your nephew kidnapped by a crazed drunk? I don't think so."

The words "crazed drunk" stung Angelo, but he knew that it was true. She was helpless in the face of Vincenzo's rage. Nevertheless, family is family right or wrong. "I understand, Clelia, but the fact remains that Vincenzo for all his faults did not deserve to die such a humiliating death."

Her voice was raised, "That was not my fault, Angelo. The police have said so."

"Be that as it may, Clelia, we want to put this dreadful matter behind us just as you do, but to do so, your being here would only be a constant reminder of a dark period in our family history." Angelo was becoming irritated at this discussion, and wanted to end it and leave.

"What am I to do, Angelo? I have no money; where can I go? The Poor House?"

"No, Clelia, we will help with the rent for the first six months, and after that, you will be on your own. We have hired Nurse Bartolo to help you with the transition. She should be along momentarily. For now, I must go. Please keep us informed of your progress. I wish you well." With that, Angelo turned and left, leaving Clelia shaking in the doorway.

She could not believe what had just transpired. "They are throwing me out into the street, and at the same time, wishing me well. They are hypocrites and cowards." She spat out the last words. She sat on the edge of her bed and cried despite her anger at the brothers, and at Vincenzo. "I wish I had never given in to him. Now look at me," she said to her bedroom mirror image. The mirror reflected her tired, worn appearance as tears streamed down her face.

Just then, there was a knock on the door. "Clelia, it's Nurse Bartolo. May I come in?" Clelia quickly opened the door and threw herself into the nurse's arms. "Oh, what am I going to do? Where do I go?"

"Don't worry my friend. Together we will find a path forward. Now, let's calm down, feed Felice, and we can go from there."

Chapter 36

April 21,1918. It became clear that this departure would be more than just leaving an apartment. Clelia had to face her fears, allowing herself to be deceived by Vincenzo and her growing hatred of the brothers. She and Nurse Bartolo visited the numerous aid organizations serving the burgeoning number of Italian immigrants in search of their place in the city where the "streets were paved in gold," only to discover the sad reality of overcrowded tenements, low wage jobs, street crime and destitution. At one of the city "missions," the pair learned that before Clelia could rent an apartment, she needed to be married and supported by a working husband.

"I don't ever want to marry again!" she exclaimed to one rental agent.

His response was the same that Clelia and Nurse Bartolo heard over and over. "Well, in that case, I can't help you, and I imagine that will be the same for other rental agents. Return with a husband, and we will be happy to find an apartment for you."

Angry and discouraged, Clelia returned to the apartment. "I will die first before I marry. Men manipulate women and then toss them on the trash heap of lost and desperate women, and then move on to their next victim. I won't find myself in that trap again."

"Not all men are such deviants. There are good men. We need to find a man who will be good to you, provide for you and Felice, and protect you. I shall consult with the local marriage bureau to start the search. Do you agree, Clelia? I cannot do this without your help."

Clelia did not respond. She was struggling with the whole idea of another man, a husband.

"Clelia? What is your answer? I need your agreement to proceed."

Still no response. Her face twisted as she shook her head.

Nurse Bartolo took that to mean that Clelia had made her decision. "Very well, Clelia, there is nothing more that I can do for you." She turned and made her way to the door. As she opened it…

"Wait! …I'll do it," was all that Clelia said.

"I will call on you tomorrow morning. In the meantime, I will speak to a marriage broker," the nurse said as she closed the door.

It would be a long, sleepless night for Clelia.

Chapter 37

April 22, 1918. The morning came too quickly for Clelia. First, she said her morning prayers, followed by making breakfast for her and Felice. It was during breakfast that Nurse Bartolo was banging on the door. "Clelia, I have good news!"

Clelia opened the door to see the nurse with a handful of papers, and her ever-present medical bag. Felice, by now, recognized his "Auntie Anna." He ran over to her and wrapped his arms around her leg. "My dear Felice, it's so good to see you. I have a surprise for you too." The nurse reached into her bag and produced a handful of chocolate sweets. Clelia frowned but not seriously, "Anna, his teeth will rot."

"Nonsense, it is exactly what he needs: a sweet start to his day following two women around all day in the city. What could be worse or boring?"

Clelia laughed, "Felice, only this once. No more sweets."

"Of course, mama, no more sweets," he replied tongue in cheek. Felice knew that Nurse Bartolo had an endless supply of sweets in her bag that he assumed were its only contents.

"Come, sit, let me show you what I have found." She spread out the papers on the table to reveal numerous biographies of available men in the Italian community. There were 10 individual pages, some with photographs. Each page described individual height, weight, level of education, current employment, the circumstances of their situation, and, of course, the amount in their respective bank accounts. The two women poured through the biographies obtained from the local marriage broker. Nurse Bartolo read each entry out loud, which prompted numerous and mostly funny remarks by the two women. "Isn't this fun?" the nurse exclaimed. "It is like shopping in a Sears Roebuck catalog." Clelia gave only a half-hearted grin.

The marriage broker would not allow male hopefuls to be paraded in front of the women. It was agreed that they would interview one man at a time, and not on the same day. They could take all the notes they wanted, and could ask any questions but none about sex.

Clelia and Nurse Bartolo interviewed five over the course of a month. After each meeting, the two women would discuss the prospect's potential as a husband. In the course of the meetings, both women found that they were always in agreement on the individual.

They decided on one candidate, Antonio Rocco, as the best of an uninspiring group of possibilities. There was no photograph of him, only a detailed explanation of his credentials as a future husband. He was of average height, strong build, and a farmer in Italy prior to his migration to the US. His education was minimal, but on the other hand, he had a respectable amount of money in the bank. He was currently working on the underground railroad in New

York City – steady employment, which was a plus. Antonio was a widower with one daughter, Rosalina. He admitted that he was looking more for companionship than romance, and a caring mother for Rosalina.

It was agreed that they would meet with Antonio Rocco. Three days later, both women and Felice found themselves in the office of the marriage counselor. As they entered the inner office of the counselor, they found that Antonio was already there. He rose as the marriage counselor made the introductions. Clelia noted that this was a rough-hewn man who had experienced a hard life, first as a conscript in the Italian army, then as a farmer during the worst period of drought in Italy's recorded history, the death of his wife, and now a tunnel worker with a young daughter. He spoke softly, almost in a whisper. "I cannot be a tunnel worker and care for a child, especially not a daughter." Clelia acknowledged his words with a nod and gentle smile. It was Felice, in his childlike innocence, that broke the ice. "Mr. Antonio, will you be my papa?"

Antonio was apologetic. "I would like to continue this meeting, but I must return to the tunnel lest I lose pay for the day. Perhaps, we could meet again in the evening. I would like you to meet my daughter, Rosalina." Nurse Bartolo was not keen on the idea. "A lady should not be out at night unaccompanied." But Clelia felt a pang of sympathy for him, "Yes, an evening meeting is acceptable." Nurse Bartolo frowned but also realized that Clelia was interested in pursuing the matter. A date and time were agreed upon. Antonio rose to his feet, bowed his head and said, "Thank you for meeting with me today. I shall look forward to our next meeting." As he turned to leave, he bent over and whispered something in Felice's ear that prompted a wide grin from the child. When asked, Felice demurred, "Mama, it's a secret."

Chapter 38

June 8, 1918. After two successive meetings, it was agreed that Antonio and Clelia would marry. At the same time, at Clelia's insistence, the marriage would only be one of companionship, mutual support and protection. Unspoken but understood: there would be no sex.

As both Antonio and Clelia were widowed, the Catholic Church consented to the hastily arranged marriage. There would be none of the pomp of a conventional marriage ceremony. The wedding was only attended by Nurse Barolo. The Talarico brothers were not invited. This was, after all, a marriage of convenience: Clelia and Felice needed stability and security; Antonio needed someone to look after him and Rosalina.

Despite the stories, life in Little Italy was harsh. Poverty, crime and the hostilities imported from the "old country" made life on Mulberry Street uncertain. It was agreed that she and Felice would move into Antonio's apartment located in a neighborhood that came to be known as "Harlem" on 123rd Street. There were only three rooms, one bedroom, a combination living room and a kitchen. The bedroom became Clelia's; everyone else slept in the living room. In summer, the heat and humidity were oppressive; in winter, it was so cold that the windows froze on the inside panes. Even the rats took shelter from the cold in the apartment.

The years passed agonizingly slowly for Clelia. The routine never varied: Antonio rose before sunrise for work; Clelia spent her days cooking, washing clothes by hand and looking after Felice and Rosalina. Nurse Bartolo, previously a constant visitor to meet Clelia and her "nephew" Felice, now rarely visited. Clelia was not clear why the visits were so infrequent. Perhaps it was guilt for facilitating this harsh marital arrangement. Antonio was kind, generous and loving to both children; he could not, however, pierce the veil of Clelia's anger, cynicism and despair. After a while, that veil became Clelia's face. She became hard, demanding and belligerent. Regardless of what Antonio did for his family, it was never enough and he was constantly met with derision and insults.

Clelia plunged deeper into depression. She abandoned the Catholic Church forever. She never again entered a church until her own funeral. She despaired of everything, except Felice. He was her remaining hook to reality. But even that reality was also marred by an internal conflict. She wanted to love her son, but he was a constant reminder of Vincenzo's perfidy. Her anger turned to a fury that burned in her stomach at the thought of what could have been.

Within a few short years, Antonio and Clelia rarely spoke to each other, and then only when Clelia berated him. Despite the assumptions which underlined the marriage, there was no companionship, and support was minimal on both sides.

The relationship, if one could call it that, became a prison for both parties. Neither could leave the marriage. Clelia needed to maintain the façade of a housewife, mother and wife, and Antonio's pretense was as a responsible and devoted provider who needed to work two jobs to put food on the table.

Before too long, they had come to hate one another.

Chapter 39

Both Felice and Rosalina had grown apart. Whereas Felice had grown up as an intense and often times morose child, Rosalina, older than Felice by five years, was a happy, jovial child. She could amuse herself without interacting with any member of the family. There was little filial contact between them. As a result, the four people in the Rocco household were complete strangers who occupied the same space.

Both Felice and Rosalina were bullied in school, she because of her weight, and he for being unfriendly and distant. She reacted by eating more; he reacted by retreating into himself. Neither was a particularly good student – both would never finish high school. Despite their lack of meaningful education, they were both "street smart" and knew how to navigate their way with hustlers, over-charging retailers, and the ever-present heroin dealers.

As Rosalina was the older of the two, she was sent to work at the age of fifteen in a sweatshop. She would work in dress shops for the remainder of her life. What meager pay she received, she turned over to Clelia, as did Antonio, and later Felice. Rosalina had one failed love affair that resulted in her remaining single for the remainder of her life.

Felice's teenage years could only be described as aimless. He had little enthusiasm for school and work, and he went through several jobs before the events of December 7th, 1941 changed the course of his life. He dropped out of high school only to finish later in his life.

He met a lovely young girl, named Josefina. After an arranged first date, he was smitten. It turned out to be a rocky road to love from the outset. Her only offense was that she was Sicilian. Clelia forbade her son to associate with "those scourges from Sicily". Despite her remonstrations regarding Sicilians, she was, of course, in a losing contest. In the waning years of his military service, he would eventually marry Josefina, his first and only date, when he was 22. For Josefina, Felice was her first love. However, for him, it was his escape, more to leave home than out of any sense of love. After several years, the marriage was something of a success despite the dark personality he had become.

It was on June 14th, 1942 that he along with millions of other young men received the notice of conscription. The notice began with **"Greetings, you are commanded to report to a processing center for military service."**

He said a final goodbye to his mother. He left his home early morning, and by the end of the day, found himself on a troop train bound for the Great Lakes Naval Training Center. With his departure, he left Clelia with Antonio and Rosalina. He would never return to his childhood home on 123rd Street. Clelia was devastated at the news of his conscription and subsequent departure. She recalled World War I and the death of so many young boys. They were now calling this World War II. Although he wrote the occasional letter to her from his duty station, it didn't mitigate her fear and anxiety for her only child. She redoubled her prayers, but she never cried. Clelia's heart was becoming as barren and shriveled as a dry river bed.

Felice was assigned as a fireman aboard a naval aircraft carrier, and later as an instructor at the naval fire school. At the end of the war, he was honorably discharged after four years in service. The war and his assignments changed the man-boy into a man.

The first order of business upon his return was to marry Josefina. Typically, at church weddings, the respective families are seated on opposite sides of the main aisle. While the Sicilian contingent was there in full force for Josefina, there were only three people on Felice's side: Clelia, Antonio and Rosalina. The Sicilian side was thrilled at the marriage of an Italian immigrant; Felice's side remained silent and morose. None of Felice's family attended the after-wedding party, and Felice didn't care.

When they got home, Clelia, Antonio and Rosalina picked up where they left off prior to the wedding: sitting in silence, each with their own thoughts. Dinner that evening consisted of pasta with something resembling cauliflower floating in a red sauce. The black spots on the cauliflower did not put them off from eating. Spoiled vegetables were part of their weekly diet.

Chapter 40

May 11, 1945. Felice purchased a three-story house with the help of the GI Bill, which would provide returning soldiers with a mortgage. Within 24 hours after the purchase, and without prior notice, Clelia, Antonio and Rosalina moved in with their meager belongings. At the same time, Felice's in-laws, a family of four, moved in to occupy the third floor. The Roman contingent occupied the lower two floors; the Sicilians were on the third. It would be a caldron that boiled over on many occasions, largely instigated by Clelia, such was her animus toward

Sicilians. Dinners consisted of a momentary truce as both groups ate together, after which the battle lines were re-drawn. To the relief of Felice and Josefina, after several turbulent years, the Sicilian family decamped to another apartment.

Clelia now found herself in a new role: the chatelaine of the family household, a role which included cooking, cleaning and washing. After three children, her role included raising them as both parents worked long hours to support their growing family, Clelia, Antonio and Rosalina. The children became the center of her attention, but nothing could change her hostility toward the world, and that was reflected in the treatment of the three children. She was unforgiving, unsmiling and harsh with the two brothers, while the girl, the youngest of the three, was treated with special care. As a result, one brother became a manic depressive; and the second one became an introvert with a stutter. Only the girl survived the trauma, but she too bore the scars of years of reprimand and disapproval. Any attempt to show affection was generally met with a scowl.

For Clelia, the years passed agonizingly slowly. She rarely spoke and kept to herself, sitting sullenly by a window with her ever-present rosary beads. She had no friends and desired none. She was becoming increasingly disconnected from the day-to-day interactions of family members. At the dinner table, she spoke only when spoken to, and even then only in Italian. Clelia was sinking slowly into a void where no one could reach her. No one, not even Felice, could penetrate the shell that surrounded her.

Her face spoke of her emptiness. Her hair had gone completely white, which she always wore in a tight bun that made her appear more severe. The lines on her face were evidence of the years of anger, hostility and hatred. Her eyes did not hide her animus. When her three grandchildren had grown and left home, Clelia became even more isolated from the outside world. Their occasional visits home were a testament to that isolation. After the usual courtesies of "hello" and "goodbye", Clelia retreated into her distant safe space accompanied by complete silence. Despite understanding English after so many years, she refused to enter into any discussion.

Antonio was treated with disdain. Any attempt by Antonio at even the most banal conversation was met with a dismissive wave or silence. More often than not, interactions between them were reduced to hurling abuse at one another and heated arguments over the simplest matters like how much salt to put in a sauce. The forbearing Antonio had been completely ostracized from her life. He spent the remainder of his days doing the family shopping and lovingly tending his garden and a fig tree. He died as he lived: peacefully and quietly. Clelia never shed a tear.

# Chapter 41

January, 1973. The winter was bitter; the temperature remained below freezing for several weeks and mounds of snow made many roads impassable for days. For reasons known only to him, Felice moved to a small village upstate New York; Josefina never challenged his decision, such was her loyalty. Rosalina had become seriously ill; she was moved into a care home which she never left until her death. Clelia was now living alone with her son and daughter-in-law. As she sat by her bedroom window, her reflection told a story of a woman who had stopped caring.

She was a shell, gaunt and withered. Nothing mattered any longer. She rarely spoke, ate very little and rarely changed out of her bedclothes. Her journey was coming to an end. She knew it, and silently welcomed it. Her only companion was the ever-present statute of the Sacred Heart, and her rosary beads that accompanied her throughout the years.

One evening upon his return from work, Felice stood by the entrance to her room. "Hello, mama. How are you today?" There was no reply. Her head was bowed down to her chest. Her hands on her lap were entwined by her rosary beads. "Hello, mama," Felice repeated. She remained motionless. Her eyes were closed and her hands were cold. Her mouth was slightly open as if she were praying.

She was dead.

A mandatory autopsy revealed that but for poor nutrition, she was an otherwise healthy woman at the age of 95. The coroner was at a loss to find a cause of death. On the death certificate, for want of a real cause, he attributed it to heart failure. However, the truth spoke of something far more depressing: she had given up on life. Clelia surrendered to death as a welcome escape. She yielded to a barren and wretched existence, absent joy or fulfillment, a place where love was denied from her.

At both her wake and funeral, only Felice, Josefina, and her three grandchildren, Felice Jr., Ricardo, and Clelia were in attendance. This was the sum of her world, another sad commentary on a life lost. No one remembered the earnest young woman who had bravely left the harsh life of the Vatican orphanage to find a job in an Italian travel agency; the happy young woman in a Rome restaurant whose surrogate father showered her with love and affection. All that happiness was lost when an ambitious and unscrupulous man charmed his way into her life, took advantage of the loss of her beloved father, and went on to rape her. One moment in time collapsed her world.

She was consigned to an inconspicuous grave in a small overcrowded cemetery in Wurtsboro, New York. A small gravestone was a sad testament to a lost life. It simply read, "Clelia Rocco, died March 17, 1973". The grave marker is now all but lost in the tall grass where a gentle spring breeze whispers a monologue of sadness.

Epilogue

Many years later, on a grey morning in Rome, a lone man stopped in front of the door to the Vatican convent. He was carrying a small bouquet of daisies which he placed on the threshold. He then knocked gently on the door.

The door monitor, Sister Almerina, answered only to find the bunch of flowers. Attached was a note that read, "Grandma, We love you. Rest in peace". It was signed, "Felice, Ricardo, Clelia."

Domenico's restaurant is still a well-known feature on Mulberry Street.

About the Author

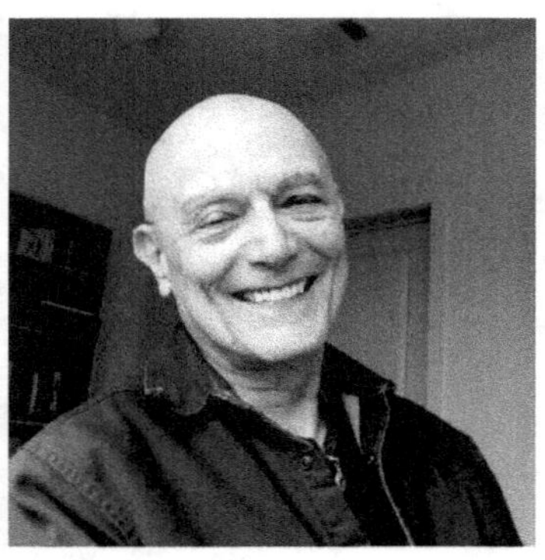 **Philip Antony** has drawn on his experiences from his multi-faceted career as a lawyer, business consultant and university professor. He has travelled the world where he was privileged to meet and interact with people of many cultures, which he has woven into all of his stories. He has produced a long line of young adult stories and adult novels in which his rich imagination and international experiences have created a cast of colourful, relatable characters and exciting adventures.

The underlying theme of his stories is the power of love, friendship and compassion that overcome the forces of hatred and division. Although his stories are works of fiction, his novels convey that contemporary message with excitement interspersed with warmth and humour. His work stands in stark contrast to the enmity and divisiveness we read about in our world today.